I0757853

Published by: Cinnabar Moth Publishing LLC
Santa Fe, New Mexico

Cover Design by: Ira Geneve

ISBN-13: 978-1-953971-38-8
Library of Congress Control Number: 2022933065

The Secrets that Kill Us

PHOENIX BLACKWOOD

Dedication:

To those of you who feel alone or too broken to be loved -- you're perfect. Keep fighting and love will come.

Content Notes:

The Secrets that Kill Us deals with many difficult topics that may be triggering for some readers. Most of the topics are implied while a few are explicit.

Childhood sexual abuse (implied)
Sexual assault (implied)
Drug use (explicit)
Intravenous drug use (explicit)
Alcohol use/abuse (explicit and implied)
Child abuse (explicit and implied)
Explicit language
Homophobia (explicit)
Homophobic slur
Suicide (explicit)
Self harm (head banging)
Bullying (explicit)

Prologue

Fluorescent lights flickered overhead, making me squint even more than usual to try and see everything going on around me. The air smelled of overripe fruit; just looking at the tables in the crowded classroom made me feel sticky. Trying to ignore the stares of students as I walked by them, I made my way to the back corner of the class and sat down. I started squirming in my seat due to the texture on the desk's surface – it was like someone had spilled a cup of fruit juice and let it dry there. A few kids looked back at me and snickered. I was the new kid *again*, and fifth grade in this school would probably be just as ruthless, if not more so, than in the others.

The teacher called attention to the front of the classroom. I couldn't see what was going on from the back, but I didn't really care. It was only a matter of time before they would place me in easier classes when they realized that I had no idea what was happening in any of the standard ones. I'd already been held back a year, what's the point of trying now? Everyone already assumed I wouldn't succeed. Trying harder just got me a headache and sometimes worse grades. I loosely paid attention as the teacher droned on about decimals and how to multiply them, which was funny because I still barely knew the difference between a fraction and a decimal. One's a dot and the other's a slash, I had no idea which one was which.

The bell rang for lunch, and I made my way towards the cafeteria. A few kids pushed past me on the way there, almost knocking me over. I'd always been pretty small, easily lost in the sea of children in the hallways. I stared at the ground as I walked, the dingy, blue-speckled tiles providing a sliver of entertainment in an otherwise overall beige hallway. The cafeteria didn't smell great, it had a type of fast-food scent with a hint of sweaty preteen to it. Grabbing a dry-looking piece of pizza and a bottle of water while in line, I went to sit at an empty table in the corner of the room. It was quieter there, the general buzz of conversation was overwhelming my ability to think. I got as far in the corner as I could, facing the room. No one could sneak up on me here. The pizza felt as dry in my mouth as it had looked, and I squinted while trying to chew my way through it.

Much to my surprise, a girl came up to the table and sat across from me. She looked at me with a warm smile, and I glanced at her briefly before looking back down at my tray. She was pale and had dirty blond hair, almost looking like a ghost next to my freckled brown skin. Her eyes were the brightest green I'd ever seen, and she was wearing a light-yellow sundress with a bow in the back. She seemed so comfortable in the environment, sitting in the middle of the bench, not caring who was behind her. Her gaze fell on me as if she was unaware that anyone else was in the room.

"You're new." Her voice was soft and warm, just like her smile that curled up on the edges, almost like a cat's.

I didn't say anything. Instead, I stared down at the pizza and attempted to rip off another bite. She let out a small giggle and I looked up at her, not sure if she was laughing at me or how ridiculously shitty this pizza was.

"I'm Alex."

I tipped my head up at her slightly to acknowledge the greeting, still unsure of her motive.

"You should really avoid the pizza on Fridays, they just cook a huge batch on Monday so it's the same reheated crap for the rest of the entire week. That slab you've got there has been reheated at least four times."

I looked back down at the tray. It seemed impossible to make pizza that dry, so her explanation made sense. I looked back at her and narrowed my eyes, still wary of how friendly she was being. After her kindness, I figured I should at least give her my name.

"Liz." The word gruffly escaped my mouth.

"Oh, so you *can* talk! I was starting to wonder." She let out another giggle, hunkering down in the seat and beginning to pick at the limp French fries she had on her tray.

I pushed the pizza away. My jaw hurt from trying to get through the two bites I had taken. Plastic scraped on the table, and I looked over to see the girl pushing her tray closer to me. Her food selection didn't look a lot better, but it didn't look like my teeth would fall out trying to eat it. There were the soggy-looking French fries, some yellowish apple slices, and some chicken nuggets that probably weren't even real chicken.

"We can share."

I still didn't understand why she was being nice to me, but I felt a sharp pain in my stomach as it grumbled, begging for something to subsist on. Picking up one of the apple slices,

I muttered, "Thanks," as I bit into it. The gratitude was barely audible to myself over the chatter of the room.

She smiled at me again. "People are usually jerks to the new kids, especially halfway through the year. We can be friends if you want, I'll at least try not to be a jerk."

The end of her sentence had a slight sarcastic tone to it, but she seemed genuine enough. I was still looking for any ulterior motive she would have for talking to me. Something told me that she liked the project of winning over the gloomy outsider.

"Okay." I conceded.

She held out a hand. "That means we look out for each other. I've got your back, you've got mine."

Shaking her hand, I avoided eye contact. If only she knew how much trouble I'd be.

CHAPTER ONE

High school wasn't much different than middle school, other than things being less sticky and more dingy. I'd made it through freshman year by the skin of my teeth, and now the daunting task of sophomore year stood before me, halfway accomplished. The guys were a lot more obnoxious, graduating from senseless teasing to aggression in order to fulfill their newfound need for overbearing toxic masculinity. I rolled my eyes as I walked past a group of guys pushing each other around, proving my point. At least I wasn't the new kid this time. I'd somehow managed to keep up with the class and graduate. I'd made it through a year and a half of high school without being held back. It was still a constant struggle. When I got to my locker I squinted at the paper I'd been given for the code, bringing it closer to my face. Contacts weren't cutting it, I really needed to wear my glasses. But damn, did I hate them. After a few different attempts I managed to get the right numbers and threw the books I didn't need in. They made a loud slam as they hit the back of the locker.

Another metallic thud, a few feet away this time. There was another group of boys pushing each other around. My eyes rolled until I heard a shout from a kid I couldn't even see. I craned my neck to get a look. He was on the ground, and the group of kids was focused on him. As I narrowed my eyes, one of the bigger guys kicked the kid in the stomach. My blood boiled. I threw my bag to the ground and walked over to them, pushing the guy that had thrown the kick out of the way. He slid back and hit the locker.

"What the fuck?!" His face turned a bright red as he faced me.

"Leave him the fuck alone." I warned, my tone flat.

"Stay out of this, bitch." He shoved me and I took a step back to steady myself.

Furrowing my eyebrows, I clenched my fists tight enough that my nails dug into my hand. I took a step forward and with one swift movement I punched him square in the face.

"Fuck!" He yelled.

His shout was muffled through his hands that were covering his nose. A small amount of blood dripped down through his fingers, tears in his eyes to go along with it. Rage flashed across his face, and a couple of his friends tried to grab me and hold me down. I ducked as hands flew towards me and he charged. I simply stepped out of the way, causing him to overshoot and hit the lockers on the other side of the hall. Cursing, he got up and stumbled away, giving up the fight. The group followed, but not without pushing me into the lockers.

I steadied myself and then looked down at the kid that the group had been ganging up on. He was curled up with his knees to his chest, his arms covering his face and head. He was shaking. This was the part I wasn't good at. Pushing around hardheaded bullies was nothing, I'd been doing that all my life. Comforting the victim was something I didn't stick around for, since it was usually me. I didn't need comforting.

I knelt down next to him and tried to soften my voice. "You okay?"

As he unburied his face, I saw that he had long, messy black hair tied up in a ponytail and deep brown eyes. His skin was pale, but his face was flushed from breathing heavily. Maybe he'd been crying, but I couldn't tell since he was now quiet and the fringe of his hair cast shadows on his face. Overall, his physique was pretty small – he was taller than me, but that didn't take much. Most people were taller than my whopping 5'2". There was a bit of blood on the corner of his mouth and bruises on his arms, some yellowed with age and some fresh. This clearly wasn't the first time the kid had gotten beaten on.

"Yeah…" His voice was shaky.

I stood up and offered him a hand that he hesitantly took. He wobbled and leaned against the lockers, his face losing its flush and growing pale to match the rest of him.

"You should go to the nurse, you don't look great."

"No…no, it's fine. I don't…" His voice trailed off. There was apprehension in his voice. Straightening his posture using the lockers for support, he looked at me for the first time. "Thanks…I'm okay."

He was waving me off with his words - I couldn't help him if he didn't want it. So, I gave him a half smile and picked up my books, putting up a hand to wave as I left. I made my way down the hallway until after a few turns I came upon an open locker and a girl sifting through the items inside. Stopping there, I leaned against the locker next to her.

Her once dirty blond hair was now dyed a bright, fiery red. It suited her better, and she'd done her eyebrows to match.

She'd grown much taller than me and her lanky frame had gotten much fuller. Her piercing green eyes were still just the same. Once we'd hit high school, she'd started accenting them with makeup. She didn't overdo it – a simple cat-eye eyeliner and a bit of smoky eyeshadow. To a similar effect, she wore some red-tinted lip gloss. The corners of her mouth still curved up a bit, even though she wasn't smiling right now.

Actually, she looked pretty pissed. Her eyebrows were furrowed, and she slammed her locker shut before she even noticed I was there. The word *"Slut"* was carved in the front of it.

The familiar heat washed over me, a sensation that begged for action. "Who do I gotta beat up?"

She glared at me, a look that made my stomach drop. "What's that?" She asked, nodding towards my hand.

For the first time since the scuffle earlier, I looked at my hand. My knuckles were raw and there was a smattering of blood across the back of my hand. Not mine. I hadn't noticed.

"Some kids were being dicks." I looked down at the ground, not wanting to face the intensity of the daggers she was staring in my direction.

Why is she mad at me?

"You know that's not the way to handle it. You got away with a lot of shit in middle school you can't do here. It's a wonder you haven't gotten more than suspensions. You're practically on your last strike. Learn to walk away." Her eyes were narrowed at me, misplaced anger wavering slightly across her face.

I couldn't help but roll my eyes. "How do you expect me to walk away when people are getting hurt?"

"That's such an excuse. Stop fighting other people's battles. Care about yourself for a change."

She didn't like me fighting, but this wasn't anything new. It was pretty much the only fight we'd ever had in our four years of friendship. A battle she always lost with me.

Something else had to be wrong, especially since she was dodging the topic of her locker. She knew I didn't make a good punching bag, so the hostility she threw in my direction wasn't typical and made my stomach churn and my throat feel tight. I looked down at the ground again, shuffling my foot across the tile it had been resting on.

She inhaled sharply and let the breath out slowly. "Sorry...I got in a fight with my mom this morning. And this shit." She gestured towards her locker. When she looked back at me, the daggers were gone, replaced with upturned eyebrows and pleading eyes. "You really need to stop though, you're the only thing in my life that's not fake and I don't want to lose that"

There was a look of genuine sadness on her face. I wanted to run my hand down her cheek, but that felt like crossing the boundaries of friendship. Instead, I gave her a half smile. She'd never gotten along with her mom very well. Things had been especially tense lately – the locker was probably more of a reminder of that than a dig at her character. She'd been with a different boy almost every week since high school started, and her mom blamed that for all of her problems. Her mom never considered the alternative, that Alex was looking for the love she didn't get at home.

"Let's go get lunch," I offered, trying to distract her.

She huffed a little, knowing what I was doing, but let it happen anyway and started walking in the direction of the cafeteria. Catching up to her, I stayed quiet. I hated that I didn't know how to fix things for her.

We both grabbed food from the line – she had a limp salad and I grabbed a pretty generic sandwich. Food wasn't any better here than it had been in middle school. We sat at a corner table, and I still sat as close as I could to the wall. Somehow Alex never seemed to mind turning her back to the entire room – she was able to focus as though we were the only two people there. She shook up her salad and then started picking at the wilted leaves.

"So what was happening this time?" Alex nodded at my hand again. "I know you never pick the fight."

My shoulders bounced. "Assholes were ganging up on a kid. Wasn't even fighting back."

She shook her head. "Always so noble."

I rolled my eyes.

Looking around the room, she pointed at a guy in a red t-shirt a few tables away. "He wasn't one of them, was he?"

"No. Why?"

"You keep telling me I should be more picky, so I guess weeding out bullies is a good start."

I looked down at the table. Another fling. Someday she'd get hurt.

She snickered under her breath. "How come you've never dated? If you put in the teeniest bit of effort you'd be able to get any guy you want." She gently pulled my long, deep-brown ponytail over my shoulder and dropped it. "You're gorgeous."

My face got *so* hot, and my skin crawled a little. Something about her saying that made me feel tingly inside. My curves didn't suit me as well as hers did – at least I didn't think so. My chest had grown heavy, which didn't do anything but hurt my shoulders and attract attention that I despised. I wore oversized sweatshirts to negate the latter issue. Because I exercised pretty frequently, I had a muscular frame that my wide hips tried to contradict. My hair was long only because I hated the idea of sitting in a chair while someone stood over me with a pair of scissors. The only feature I didn't hate was my strong jawline, but that was the only one guys weren't keen on.

She was right, I could get any guy I wanted. Problem was, I didn't want any *guy*.

"You could do literally anything with your hair and then wear clothes that actually fit. Boom. Boyfriend. You wouldn't even need makeup!" She said, waving her fork in the air.

I shrank down in my seat. "Just never liked anyone." My eyes pleaded with her to change the topic.

She laughed. "Who says you have to actually like them? You're the most cynical person I've ever met, you can't tell me you buy into that 'true love' bullshit. Let me set you up with someone."

I didn't answer. I didn't know how to answer.

Studying me, she tried to find a reaction to what she'd said. Her face looked almost as confused as I felt.

Giving up, she shook her head again. "Sometimes I don't get you."

Exhaling sharply, I pushed aside the sandwich I hadn't even touched. My stomach hurt. I was done with today.

Alex turned her attention to the room and smiled, waving as a tall, skinny blond walked by. I looked up, then back down again. It was Seth – my adopted brother. He was a junior, and we pretended not to know each other at school. He and I looked so drastically different that just knowing we were from the same family, people would know that at least one of us was adopted. He was tall and lanky, with deep blue eyes and the lightest blond hair a human could naturally have – barely a shade darker than his porcelain skin. We didn't cross paths at school often, him being a class above me, so we figured it would be easier this way. He sat down a few tables away, with a group of kids he played music with after school. They didn't even know we knew each other – he'd always go to someone else's house. Sometimes I wondered if he was embarrassed of me.

The bell rang for the end of the period, and I scooped up my bag and tray without saying anything. Alex looked at me quizzically – she was used to my silence, but she could also tell when something was off.

I floated through the rest of my classes that day. Concentrating was always hard, but today was worse for some reason. Random days were worse sometimes, thinking felt like trying to make out a far-away object through a thick fog. Trying to come out of it would just give me a headache, and I wouldn't be able to maintain any kind of clarity for very long. Instead, I just gave in to the fog and could barely remember anything that happened during the day.

After school, I skipped the bus and made my way downtown to the skate park. It was sweater weather, so my sweatshirt wasn't uncomfortable like it was in the summer. The air was crisp, and if the scent weren't so polluted with gasoline and exhaust, it would have a sweet autumn smell. The bustle of the street was overwhelming even though I'd lived in the city for four years at this point. I tried to block it out with music, but I could never listen with both earbuds in without feeling like I'd be oblivious to something dangerous. Staring at the ground while walking was a good way to not accidentally make eye contact with people on the street. The sour look on my face helped me look as unapproachable as possible. Alex often joked about how bad my resting bitch face was.

I rubbed my hands on the wood grain on the bottom of my skateboard as I walked – it was a nice feeling, one that was familiar and soothing. Skating was probably the only positive activity I'd engaged in consistently since I was around ten. "Positive" was subjective, I guess. Mom always reprimanded me because I refused to wear a helmet. The characters that hung around the park weren't great, but most would consider me one of the bad ones anyway. I came upon the chain-link fence that enclosed the skate park and walked in, dropping my board on the ground.

Skating around obstacles, I felt a little calmer as the wind blew against my face. The low ponytail I kept my hair in fluttered as I dropped down ramps and went over jumps. I was still intensely aware of how many people were around me, but I felt more untouchable when I was moving through the park on my board. The sun started to lower in the sky, and I slowed down to take a break.

"Hey!" Someone yelled across the park. My head snapped in the direction of the sound, and I saw a recognizable figure approaching me. This time, his jet black hair was brushed out of his face in a bun on top of his head. He'd cleaned up the blood that had been running down his mouth. There wasn't any hiding how bruised his arms were, though. I stopped and watched him as he approached.

"Thank you, y'know, for earlier."

I gave him a nod in acknowledgement. He seemed a lot more confident in this setting – his shoulders back as he stood up straight to face me, rather than hunched over as he'd been earlier.

"I'm Jeremy. It's weird I've never seen you before – that's a nice-ass board and you skate like you've been at it for a while."

I shrugged. "Thanks."

Thinking back, I had seen him here a few times before – I'm always acutely aware of what people were around me. I didn't tend to retain that information for later encounters.

"It's Liz." Giving him my name felt appropriate since he'd done the same.

"Sorry, I kinda brushed you off earlier, it's just that every time I go to someone things get so much worse."

Blinking at him, the gears in my head started to turn. I knew the signs.

"C'mere." I said, nodding in the direction of a bench towards the back of the park.

He raised an eyebrow, but followed and sat down with me anyway. I leaned my board against the bench and sat cross-legged. He apprehensively set his board next to mine – his looked decent – not a cheap department store board, but not as polished and cared for as mine.

He was careful about leaving space between us when he sat, like he was trying to avoid sitting too close. His cheeks were slowly turning a light red. Retaining a stiff and straightened posture, he appeared more bashful than afraid. I chanced a few glances at his arms without him noticing. On top of the bruises, I could see random darkened circles along his forearms. They were small, and some healed over, but others looked fairly recent.

"Seems like you're smart enough to avoid those shitbags outside of school." I pressed.

He looked at me questioningly.

"So how'd you get those?" I gestured towards the burn marks.

Immediately, he shifted on the bench and pulled his sleeves down. His posture began to slouch and he covered his arms as he stared towards the ground.

"You really don't miss shit, do you?"

I shrugged and pulled a blunt out of my jeans pocket and

a lighter out of the other. Inhaling deeply as I lit it, I passed it over to him. He didn't hesitate to take it. I exhaled slowly, blowing the smoke away from his direction.

"Mom or dad?" I asked, staring into the distance.

He exhaled and handed the blunt back to me before answering. "Mom. Dad left a long time ago."

A nod. Without looking at him, I offered, "You can stay at my house if you ever need to. I know how it is."

He looked at me, his eyebrows raised and eyes wide. I didn't think anyone had ever offered him respite before. Then again, judging by his reactions, it seemed he'd gone out of his way to not tell anyone either. How'd I get it out of him so easily?

"Th...Thanks." he muttered. "You know what it's like, huh?"

I passed him back the blunt after taking another drag, and shrugged as I exhaled. My chest wasn't the only thing I hid with oversized clothes – scars marred my entire body. My head started buzzing with thoughts I didn't want to listen to.

"How long have you skated for?" I asked as he passed the blunt back, wanting to get the attention off of me.

"Three-ish years? I was mostly looking for a way to get out of the house. How about you?"

"Six."

"Damn, no wonder you're so smooth with it."

I chuckled a little. No one had ever referred to me as smooth before, in regards to anything.

""What?" he asked.

"If you knew me, you'd never call me smooth."

He looked me up and down before responding. "Can I? Know you?"

After taking the last drag of the blunt, I stamped it out on the ground and squinted against the increasingly louder thoughts in my head.

Get out before he really sees you.

"As much as anyone, I guess."

Nodding, he leaned back into the bench. The sun was lowering in the sky, casting pink and orange across the clouds. Day crowd beginning to leave, I spotted a familiar figure in the back corner of the park.

Giving Jeremy one last glance, I stood from the bench, picking up my board. "I'll catch you later."

I put my hand up as a goodbye, and walked over to where the figure was standing. Checking my wallet, I found that I had a decent wad of cash, mostly from hustling the very same guy I was about to hand it back to. He was pacing around in the corner of the park, stopping to talk to the occasional passerby that called his attention. His focus barely shifted as I approached him and slid some money into his pocket. Handing me a small bag of white powder, he dipped his head at me while still talking to another guy. I put the bag in my pocket before turning to leave. Weed lifted the fog a little, but this would put a stop to the screaming in my head that had grown increasingly louder since I'd stopped skating.

It was dark at this point, time slipped by so quickly when I was like this. The streets were less crowded with cars on the walk home. A sour smell of gasoline still lingered in the air as I made my way down the road. After about a ten-minute walk, I arrived at a two-story house that was painted light yellow with white trim. I dug keys out of my pocket and unlocked the door, taking a step inside. The smell of stir fry hit me in the face as I shut the door.

"Hey, kid." His voice was smooth and calm.

Seth always felt the most at home in the kitchen. Thank god, because Mom couldn't even boil water. She always told me that her medical degree supported a lot of take-out and contributed to her lack of time to attempt cooking.

"Hey," I muttered.

He slid a plate of the stir fry across the counter towards me. I didn't feel like eating, but I was hungry from skipping lunch and Seth's food always smelled so damn good. Leaning my board against the kitchen island, I sat down on one of the stools. The food was sweet and spicy and full of vegetables and herbs. Seth grabbed himself a plate and sat down across from me.

We ate in silence. It wasn't that we didn't get along – Seth and I actually had a pretty good relationship. Both of us enjoyed the quiet. He knew I didn't like unnecessary chatter, and always took the time to focus on enjoying food when he ate. I finished while he still had half his plate left. After placing the dishes in the sink, I turned around and grabbed my board.

"Thanks," I said while walking upstairs towards my room.

"Mm," He answered back.

Opening the door to my room, I turned the light on. It was a floor lamp with a dim bulb. It illuminated enough of the room that I could see what I was doing, but wasn't needlessly bright. I ran my hand along the glass of my fish tank as I walked by it. The tank contained my beautiful speckled white, orange, and black koi that followed my hand. Sometimes I'd just sit and watch him for hours. I loved the way the light bounced off his scales, reflecting golden sparks back into my eyes. After putting my board down in the corner, I pulled the bag out of my pocket and set it on the desk against my wall. From my dresser, I pulled a hypodermic needle, an alcohol wipe, a spoon, and a lighter.

I set the syringe on the desk and changed into pajamas. Afterwards, I sat down and picked up the bag. As I inhaled deeply, I prepared the substance for injection and wiped my left forearm with the alcohol wipe. I pulled back on the plunger of the syringe to retrieve a dose, then injected it into my arm. Getting up to throw the syringe away, I hid it under some trash in my bin along with the bag.

My bed was a slight modification on a window seat. It was tucked into the wall against a window; the space was big enough for an entire mattress rather than some small cushions. Shelves where I kept various books, snacks, and journals lined the sides. I got into bed underneath my large down comforter that I loved because it was heavy enough to give me some calming pressure.

The drugs weren't an every night thing, I just used them on the bad days. I wasn't trying to chase some unobtainable high. In fact, I'd tried various drugs that did give me that high feeling and I hated it. It would make everything go so much faster and while it dulled some painful feelings, I'd still get overwhelmed, and it would just magnify the stress I already felt. Opiates had a different effect – they made me tired, but everything would slow down. I'd slip into a sleep where I couldn't remember the dreams. It felt like everything was on pause, if only just for a minute.

CHAPTER TWO

I awoke from the dreamless sleep as my alarm blared in the morning. Always a little groggy the morning after using, I stumbled out of bed and into the bathroom, grabbing some fresh clothes along the way. It was five AM, Seth wouldn't be up for another hour. Mom was still at work. I loved the quiet of a world still asleep, not ready to start the day. It was the best time. My mind felt a little clearer today, and I stepped into the shower feeling a little lighter than I had the day before. This is what I loved about sleeping without nightmares, everything was so calm when I woke up. Not everything rushed at me at once. The water poured over my face and felt so warm, so comforting.

As I got out of the shower, however, feelings and thoughts started to creep in. Always such a short reprieve. I shook my head as *"You're worthless"* and *"Everyone's better off without you"* pinged back and forth in my skull. I felt heavier and heavier, until everything settled into its typical slump and I opened the bathroom door, watching all the decent feelings rush out along with the steam. Sighing, I dumped my dirty clothes into the hamper in my room and sat on my bed. It was only 5:20. This was shaping up to be a long day.

I paced my room for about ten minutes before finally giving in and pulling some weed from the top drawer of my dresser. It wouldn't do much, but at least it was *something*. I'd been using more and more lately, and could feel my grip slipping on the control I pretended to have over my addiction. I couldn't use heavy stuff before school, people would be sure to notice how sluggish I was – at least Alex would. Weed didn't count, no one really cared about that, so it was the best option to tide me over until after school.

Before Seth's alarm even went off, I'd smoked an entire blunt by myself. I was a little calmer, thoughts not pinging back and forth quite so fast. But they were still there. Footsteps down the stairs – Seth would be making breakfast soon and then we'd get on the bus and it would all blur together until we were out of school. I ate the sandwich Seth whipped up and got on the bus, falling into the monotony and letting myself get lost in the routine.

———

Jeremy reluctantly followed me as we made our way through turning alleyways under the cover of the dusky sky. School had been a fog. I was looking forward to blowing off some steam.

"This is kinda shady…" he muttered behind me.

I rolled my eyes at him and kept walking. "It's just a little further."

"Where are we going, anyway?" he asked, no doubt questioning his decision to come with me without asking the details first.

He'd wanted to get out of his house, away from his mom. So I'd offered for him to tag along. I wasn't changing my plans on his account – tonight was how I made my money.

We came upon an abandoned apartment building. Run-down, boarded-up windows, the works. Jeremy glanced at me

nervously before I went up to one of the windows and kicked a
board in.

"What the – Isn't this illegal?"

"You're free to go whenever." I barely looked at him as I
slid into the space I'd made by kicking out the board.

He glanced around, rubbing his arms before finally deciding
to follow me. I helped him squeeze through and then propped the
board back up where it had been.

"Liz!" A voice called before I even turned around.

Tony. He was my dealer, but he also had enough hubris to
think he could beat me at cards every Tuesday. Most of my buying
was me handing his own money back to him.

"Who's the fresh meat?" He tipped his head in Jeremy's
direction, just as Jeremy tripped over another loose board on the
floor.

I couldn't blame him completely, as the room was dimly
lit by a lantern on the table where Tony was sitting. But damn, he
could at least pretend to be cool.

"He's chill." I assured Tony, not completely believing it
myself.

"He playing?"

"Nah." I said, grabbing a seat at the table across from him.

Two other guys sat at the table, cards already in hand. Tony
dealt me in as I leaned back into the uncomfortable folding chair,
and Jeremy found his way to a chair next to me. He looked terrified,
wringing his hands together and glancing between myself and the
other guys around the table.

This was my domain, I ruled this place.

"Ante up." Tony tossed a five in the middle of the table
and pulled out some plastic cups and a bottle of vodka. He poured

out three, leaving the fourth cup empty only for a moment before pulling out another bottle. "For the queen." He dipped his head, pouring a double shot of scotch into the empty cup.

These three had been trying desperately to beat me for over a year – at first they'd been frustrated, but at this point they were filled with pure wonder, claiming I was the only person to ever beat them. I had them all wrapped around my finger, with the bonus of free drinks as they looked for anything to throw me off my game. They should've known by then how well I held my liquor, but they just kept trying. Masculine pride is such a silly thing.

A few drinks in, I'd all but forgotten that Jeremy was there, nervously picking at his fingernails. I felt a little bad dragging him into a situation where he was clearly uncomfortable, but hey, he was free to leave at any time. Slouching down in the chair, I threw an elbow over the back and rested my wrist on it, cards lazily dangling in my hand.

My hand was terrible, but the more at ease I looked, the more intimidated these boys became. Don't get me wrong, they weren't terrible, they'd even end up taking some hands by the end of the night. I wouldn't clean them out, I'd just make some money off them. It's what would keep them coming back, begging for the chance to beat me.

When Tony pushed a high bet and I didn't fold, his face scrunched into an exasperated frown. "Fuck," he muttered, throwing his cards down. He poured me another double shot.

I waved it away, it being the fourth of the night. Even I had my limits.

He pushed the cup closer to me, bristling slightly. "You win, you drink. It's only fair."

Rolling my eyes at him, I took the cup and tossed it back. Whatever, I'd already made my money for the night. More, even. Enough to lose a bit and stroke their egos. See, you can't leave on a winning game, then they'd just get angry. No, you had to let them taste a little victory to keep them coming back. I won a couple more games because I felt like really drinking since I'd already gone over my limit, then promptly lost three in a row before stretching and yawning.

"I'm out, guys." My speech was a little slurred. I was nervous to try standing up.

Jeremy shot up out of his chair, like he'd been waiting for this moment all night. I stood up slowly, shoving the money in my pockets while leaning on the table. The room was spinning, I'd definitely had too much.

My composure was slipping away, so I made straight – well, pretty wobbly actually – for the loose board and Jeremy followed closely after me. We squeezed through and then made our way between the alleys back towards my house.

A few times, I faltered as putting one foot in front of the other became increasingly difficult. Each time, Jeremy caught me, predicting my movements. He'd done this before. I took a quick detour to puke behind a dumpster, and he was even fast enough to pull my hair out of my face before I soiled it.

Wiping my face with the back of my hand, I mustered, "You...re...re...quick."

Not really what I'd meant to say. An anxiety rose up inside me – a touch of guilt.

His mom.

That's why he was so good at this. I'd left him in virtually the same position he'd be in at home. Except, I wasn't going to hit him. One thing I'm not is an angry drunk. His expression was one of resignation as I staggered along next to him. As if he'd be doing this all his life — relationships meant taking care of drunks in return for any human contact.

I wish I could say this was the first time I'd gotten stumblingly, incoherently drunk. Far from it. Alcohol had almost always been a part of my life — my earliest memories of it were violent and messy. Back when I lived with my father, I'd finish off half-drunk whiskey bottles and wait for the world to spin. For the pain to become numb.

Now, it came second to the drugs. It didn't numb me as well and it gave me some wild dreams — God knows my brain didn't need help manufacturing horror stories to plague me with.

I was so lost in my drunken stupor that I nearly walked right into my front door, my body automatically taking me home without my mind's notice. In fact, Jeremy caught my head right as it was about to collide with the wood. The keys jumped around in my hands, the right one seemingly running away from my grasp. After the third time I dropped them, Jeremy picked them up and decided to try each one in the door. Trial and error was faster than waiting for my incoherent ass to dictate which was the right key.

A creak as the door opened. Television softly playing in the living room. Seth looked up as Jeremy closed the door behind us. I grabbed the countertop for support, squinting in the light of the kitchen. I just needed to sit down. Only for a minute.

"Nope, no, come on." Jeremy ushered me off the stool as I was beginning to slump.

Seth was suddenly at my side, not even questioning who Jeremy was. Grateful for the help in dragging me up the stairs. He was used to this too. God, was there anyone I didn't disappoint?

I fell a couple times going up the stairs, each time one of the two boys catching me. We made it to my room, and I collapsed on the bed. Seth took off my shoes while Jeremy brought over my trash can and a glass of water.

Seth started talking to Jeremy – about what I have no idea. They left my room and I gave up the fight of staying awake.

———

A dark figure followed me through a gloomy building. Broken glass crunched as I stepped over it. Turning quickly, I saw the figure dart behind the wall. I ran out the back door of the worn-down looking building. It looked as if the slightest wind would knock the whole thing over. The figure reached the doorframe while I ran through the yard. His face was warped into a scowl, and his less-than-athletic physique seemingly should have kept him from being as agile as he was while chasing me. My breath escaped me as I ran – likely both from how hard I was running and the panic setting in as my escape options dwindled. As I reached the edge of the dark woods, the trees began to feel like they were closing in on me. I tried to dodge them without losing speed, but I could hear the heavy breathing of the man behind me.

A push forward threw me off balance, and I hit the tree in front of me. Warm liquid dripped down, blood spilling out of my mouth. The metallic taste was overwhelming, but for some reason I didn't feel any pain. A grip around my ankle pulled me down to the ground. As I turned over to face the man, I threw up my legs and kicked him in the stomach as hard as I could. He let out a cough, but otherwise the blow seemed to have no effect. The figure leaned over me and grabbed me by the neck, lifting me up against the tree. I kept kicking him as hard as I could, but it seemed like he was made out of steel, his reactions minimal. His face turned into a twisted grin as I gasped for air, and he slammed my head into the tree.

"Elizabeth!" A woman's voice woke me up.

A gasp for air. My chest felt tight and my whole body shook. Mom pulled me up so that I was sitting, and I leaned against her chest, trying to catch my breath. My lip hurt now, and the metallic taste still lingered in my mouth.

"Shh…" Mom wrapped her arms around me.

My hands were cold and clammy. I was drained as I slowly started to catch my breath. She brushed my hair out of my face, and I noticed fresh scratches on her arm. I ran my hands over them as I leaned back against the wall.

"I-I'm…I'm sorry…" I still didn't have quite enough breath to speak coherently.

"You didn't mean it, it's okay sweetheart. Besides…" she looked at my lip and grabbed a tissue off my shelf to wipe away the blood, "I think you did more of a number on yourself."

Taking the tissue, I held it to my lip. It was still bleeding. Mom got up to turn the light on and then sat back down on the edge of my bed. After grabbing my glasses and putting them on, I realized that she must've just gotten home - she was still in her scrubs from work and her light-blond hair was still in the messy bun she only wore on shift. Her light-green eyes always looked dark after she'd finished a long shift – she worked in the emergency department often, so most of her nights were spent seeing some awful aspects of humanity.

"I was screaming again, wasn't I?" Pulling the tissue away from my lip, I stared at the blood stain that was slowly growing across its surface.

She nodded. "I feel like they've been getting worse, am I right?"

I shrugged. She'd tried so many times to talk me into going to a therapist, I didn't want to give her an excuse to force me to go. I'd had a mandated therapist when I was in foster care who never did anything but make me feel worse – somehow Mom was convinced that one could help me, which was a joke. All they'd ever do is pick apart how awful everything I did was, and question why I thought it was okay to do those things. My mandated therapist had managed to convince me that every home that rejected me was because I didn't want to be there. That I'd made them send me away. Part of me still felt like everything that had happened was my fault.

"I'll make you some tea, okay? Why don't you come downstairs." She got up and left my room. Her footsteps faded as she went down the stairs.

I wasn't going to be able to go back to sleep anyway, at least not without using. It was too risky to do it when she was home. Actually, it was impressive that she hadn't caught me yet.

"Shit." I muttered to myself. I reeked of alcohol. Did she not notice? Or did she not care? I'd come home shitfaced before, but only when she worked the night shift. She'd never been there to witness me stagger up to my room, and it was always straight into the shower when I woke up. Before going down the stairs, I dipped into the bathroom and gargled with some mouthwash and did my best to get rid of the smell. My balance was still off, and I was dizzy as I stumbled down the stairs. Sitting on the couch in the living room, I curled up into the oversized hoodie I'd thrown on.

Mom sat down next to me, handed me a sweet-smelling cup of chamomile tea, and flipped through the channels on the

TV. She finally stopped and leaned back with her own cup when she settled on some silly sitcom we'd watched a thousand times. There wasn't much on at this hour. She pulled her shoulder length hair out of its bun and put her feet up on the table after kicking off her shoes. I took a sip of the tea and rested my head against the back of the couch – the room was still spinning. School was going to suck tomorrow.

"Were you at a party?" The question pierced the silence that had grown comfortable between us.

"What?"

"Did you drink?"

My face flushed. Shit, she had noticed. "No."

"Don't lie to me. The smell hit me in the face the minute I walked into your room."

I didn't defend myself. There was no defense to be had.

"Alcohol can make dreams worse, you know that? You've got to be responsible with these things. I don't mind you having a little fun, but it's a school night on top of that. You have to know when to stop."

Nodding, I took another sip of the tea. It was best to just let her lecture and get it over with.

There was no lecture. "You're grounded for the week. School and then home. No Alex either."

Sure. She'd never be home to enforce that, it didn't matter. I kept quiet like I always did when she doled out her poorly-thought-through punishments. Seth had been such an easy kid. She was truly out of her depths with me. I was one of the bad ones.

I didn't get back to sleep that night. An hour or two after we sat down, Mom asked if I'd be okay if she went to bed. I was tired and my eyes hurt, but every time I closed them all I could see was the shadowy figure of a man throwing me into that tree. I hated that he still had this much control over my life. He got caught and locked up when I was six – so it had been ten years since he'd been able to put his hands on me. Yet I still saw him in the shadows and every time I went to sleep at night. Much stronger now, I could probably take him in a fight if I ever saw him again. Despite that, my brain continued to make him such a powerful figure, so untouchable regardless of anything I did. I just wanted it to stop.

When morning came, I took a long shower to try and wake up. I switched the chamomile for black tea with extra caffeine in the blend. Seth came down the stairs at around six and started rummaging through the fridge for breakfast. He didn't question why I was up – even when I did sleep, I was a morning person. I was usually up around five on a typical day. However, he could probably tell that I hadn't slept by the dark circles around my eyes – that is, if I hadn't woken him up the night before by screaming. He gave me a sympathetic smile as he pulled eggs and bacon out of the fridge. One thing we did have in common was our nightmares. He understood that part of me, being plagued by his own.

"Sandwich?" he asked as he pulled a pan out from under the sink, not addressing last night at all.

"Please." I tried to force a smile in his direction, but didn't have the energy for it. He was being sweet though, knowing breakfast sandwiches were my favorite.

We sat down and ate together before walking down the street to meet the bus. When I got on, I sat opposite from Alex – if I sat next to her she'd question why I looked like shit. She seemed to be too engulfed in her phone to notice anyway. Once the bus stopped at school, I got off and went straight to my first class without talking to her – I didn't have the energy to dodge explaining things. I didn't know how I was going to make it through the entire school day.

My first class was math, which I was notoriously bad at. I barely scraped up a passing grade, and had a hard time focusing on the lectures the teacher gave on a good day. Today was not a good day. My eyes wouldn't focus on the board and everything except the teacher's voice seemed so loud. Halfway through the class, the teacher caught me closing my eyes. He cleared his throat loudly but didn't directly address me – he might as well have, though, he was staring daggers in my direction. I wasn't well liked by teachers in general, but math was my worst subject and since the beginning of this year the teacher was convinced that I wasn't even trying. I fought through the rest of the class to keep my eyes open, trying desperately to focus on what he was saying. By the end of class, my eyes hurt even more, and I had a headache from trying so hard to concentrate.

"Elizabeth." The teacher called as I was about to leave the room.

I staggered over to his desk, not looking him in the eyes. The room suddenly felt unbearably bright, and I squinted to try and focus.

"You've got to start paying attention. You're barely passing this class, and it's required. If you fail, you'll have to retake it. Again."

I didn't argue, it would just turn into a longer speech about how I was a disappointment if I did. Instead, I just nodded.

He huffed. Clearly my nod wasn't convincing enough, he seemed to be personally offended by my lack of comprehension in his class. Like I was doing it on purpose to make him angry. Thankfully, he seemed to have given up at that moment.

"That's all." He waved me away with his hand.

I left the classroom and headed to the next one. The rest of my classes up until lunch were similar in experience, except the teachers just ignored me instead of being offended that I was struggling to stay awake. When the lunch bell rang, I inhaled deeply. Now I'd have to talk to Alex, there was no avoiding it. I walked into the lunch room – thankfully today they had macaroni and cheese. Of course it wasn't great, but it's hard to mess up stuff that comes out of a box. It was warm as well – for some reason chills had been running down my spine all day.

I sat down at the table where Alex had already taken a seat. She was buried in her phone again. Maybe I'd be off the hook – she seemed really preoccupied today. After a few minutes, she finally put her phone down and looked at me.

"Can you pick me up after my date tonight? I've got a weird feeling." Her voice was flat as she stole another glance at her phone.

My eyebrows furrowed – the fact that she was uneasy made my heart race. Most of the time her selection of guys wasn't great and she never seemed the slightest bit bothered.

"Why don't you just ditch?" I asked.

She shrugged. "He's still cute. We're going to a diner, so if you pick me up as soon as we get to his house nothing can happen. I'm probably just being overly cautious anyway."

Alex was never overly cautious.

I *really* did not like the sound of this. But I knew her well enough that I was painfully aware she'd go no matter how much I protested. Picking her up afterwards at least ensured I'd be there to protect her if shit went south.

"Sure." I muttered.

At that, she glanced up at me again and then did a double take. "You look like shit."

I snorted. "Thanks."

She didn't laugh. "You didn't sleep, did you?"

Shrugging, my eyes wandered the room.

"Liz, are you okay? You were weird yesterday too."

"I'm fine." I was trying to wave her off with my words. I ran my hand along the tray that had my food. My head still hurt and the bustle of the lunch room was making it worse, but I tried really hard not to show it. Nausea started to overcome me.

Alex shook her head at me. "We've known each other for so long and you still act like I don't know something's up. You've gotta talk to me."

No. It was my shit, and I wasn't going to make other people deal with it, especially not her. All it would get me is pity anyway, and I wasn't going to let people see me as weak. I rubbed my eyes and took a deep breath.

The bell rang, saving me. I threw out my half-eaten food and hurried to my next class, leaving Alex alone at the table.

At least I liked English – the notion was funny, considering I'd spent the majority of my childhood years refusing to speak it. The way I grew up, English spewed nothing but hate. My mom spoke to me almost exclusively in Spanish – a loving, caring language. I didn't want to embrace a language that showed me nothing but hurt. After years in the foster system with only English-speaking families, I'd finally given in when I was eight.

I sat down at my desk and tried my hardest to pay attention. With my headache growing more intense, I had to give up halfway through the class. My hands started shaking and I felt clammy. I closed my eyes – the fluorescent lights were making everything worse, and the buzzing sound they made seemed to overwhelm every other noise in the room, including the teacher. The class slowly came to an end, and I threw my books back in my bag in frustration.

Why can't I do even one thing right?

"Liz, can you come here please?" the teacher called as everyone was leaving the room. *Great.* Now I was in trouble with the only teacher that even pretended to like me. My feet slowly shuffled up to her desk. She rummaged through some papers in front of her and pulled an essay I'd written earlier in the month as well as a report I'd turned in the day before.

Fuck. Am I failing this class now too?

"So," she said as she pushed the essay towards me – it had red pen marks in the margins, but I had expected that as I'd asked if she could give me specific feedback on my writing so that I could get better. "This isn't perfect – your syntax and flow could use a bit of work. However, it's convincingly written. This is the type of work you've been giving me – you always have strong ideals and try your best to explain your line of thinking, which is almost always very logical and calculated. You've gotten me to consider some things I hadn't thought about before in some of your pieces. But this," she pushed the report forward, and some of the margin writing questioned my points in any given section. "This isn't you. Not one day have you slacked in this class, and it seemed today you couldn't hear what I was talking about."

I looked down at the floor and started running my hand back and forth on the strap of my bag.

She knows you're a fake, worthless. Incompetent.

Her expression didn't appear angry – eyebrows somewhat upturned and a squint as if she were trying to solve a puzzle. She spoke again. "So, in a roundabout way, I'm asking if you're all right."

Jig's up, she knows you're fucked up now. Broken.

She waited for a response, but I didn't give her one. She didn't know me as well as Alex, but she was perceptive and would pick up on any hint of doubt in my answer. Lying would be useless. She took a deep breath, knowing I wasn't going to say anything. Even though I liked her class, I still didn't talk a lot.

"Kiddo, you can talk to me if you need to, okay? The counselor's also here."

God damn it, why can't people leave me alone?

"I see how hard you work – I'd hate for you to lose your passion."

I mustered up the best face smile I could give her. "I'm okay, just had a long week. I'm tired."

"It's only Wednesday."

She wasn't buying it. We stared at each other awkwardly for another minute, I fidgeted with the straps and zippers on my bag while she looked me up and down. At some point, she must've given up prying. She sighed and gave me a warm smile.

"I want to see you succeed. Come see me during free period if you can."

I nodded, thanking her, and then left for my next class.

Only two more periods, then I'm done.

I was completely checked out in the last two classes. Thankfully, it seemed like the teachers were as well so they didn't notice. I got on the bus today – Alex had wanted to come over so that she could get ready for her date without her mother hovering over her. Her mom had no problem with her dating, but her expectations of Alex were very specific so she wasn't fond of most boys that Alex chose. That's the one and only point I'd ever agreed with her on. Unlike her mom, I knew Alex well enough that I didn't bother arguing – the more resistance she met the more she wanted to do something. While I didn't work well with authority, Alex's distaste was much more subtle, and she often denied it.

We both got off when the bus got to my street, and I unlocked the door, letting her go in first. No one was home – Seth had gone to a friend's and Mom had likely woken up recently and gone out to get coffee on her way to work. She had a later shift tonight so once she left she wouldn't be back until morning – my "grounding" held no consequence. I locked the door behind us and dropped my bag on the ground. Alex went to the bathroom to take a shower, leaving me alone in the kitchen. I opened the fridge, finding a plastic container with a sticky note that read "Liz" in Seth's handwriting. Opening it, I found some fresh ravioli with butter and mushroom sauce. Smiling, I heated it up, then sat down on the couch and kicked my shoes off.

When did he even have time to cook this?

I devoured the food faster than I would've liked, really wanting to enjoy the cooking. It was so damn good it was hard not to inhale it. I flipped the TV on and skimmed through the channels until Alex came out of the shower. She was wearing a frilled green blouse with short sleeves and a pair of skinny jeans. Her hair was still wet, and curled a little bit in its natural state. While she sat down on the opposite end of the couch, she set a makeup bag on the coffee table where I'd put down my dirty dish. Looking at it, Alex snickered at me.

"Didn't save me any?"

I hadn't even thought of it. Usually I did share my food with her, to the point that Seth often made a bit extra. Had I eaten all of it?

Oops.

"Sorry…" I muttered.

She laughed. "It's okay, I was messing. You haven't been eating much at school."

Thinking back to the last few days, she was right – I'd skipped lunch most times this week. Everything was a blur, she'd paid more attention than I had. Sighing, I got up and put the dish in the sink, then flopped back down on the couch. My head was heavy as I leaned back into the cushions, and I groaned when I realized I'd forgotten to take something for the pounding in my skull while I was up. The dull throbbing hadn't let up all day, it just wasn't as noticeable here because there weren't screaming fluorescent lights all over the place.

"What're you whining about?" Her tone was playful and teasing.

"My fucking head," I growled through my teeth. My hands were covering my face, so I doubt my words were understandable to anyone else.

Alex got up and grabbed a bottle of Tylenol and a glass of water. She set them on the table in front of me. It was almost creepy how well she knew me sometimes – she could understand incoherent words muttered through hands. How many unspoken cues did she notice? I leaned forward and poured three pills into my hand, then took them with a sip of water.

I sank back into the couch and looked over at Alex. She was putting makeup on – a process which I'd never understand. Her hand was so steady as she applied eyeliner. There was no doubt that I would've accidentally stabbed myself in the eye hundreds of times before I actually got anywhere if I tried.

She caught me watching her. "How come you've never tried makeup?" She asked while somehow still flawlessly applying mascara.

How do you talk while putting shit on your eyes?

"I don't like the feeling," I answered.

It wasn't a lie – I hated the texture that all the creams and powders mixed together made. I might as well be sticking my face in a bowl of wet flour.

"You'd be so gorgeous with just a little eyeliner and shadow." She cocked her head to the side, then leaned into me with a liner pencil in hand.

I threw my hands up, protecting my face. "No, c'mon."

"Please? Just let me see."

I put my hands down, too tired to argue. I sank deeper into the couch as she went to work on my face. It took her maybe ten minutes, I kept blinking and flinching each time she got close to my eyes, unintentionally making her job harder. After she finished, she leaned back with a grin on her face. Her smile was gorgeous – it had been cute the way her lips curled on the edges when she was younger. Now it brought out her full lips even more. She handed me her eyeshadow palette for the mirror.

"See? Gorgeous."

I took a look and my heart jumped against my ribcage. It didn't look bad, but it wasn't me. I hated it, but didn't have the heart to tell her. Instead, I feigned a smile while the rest of my body squirmed uncomfortably, my whole self rejecting the sight.

She shook her head and rolled her eyes at me, knowing I was faking. Returning to her own appearance, she messed with her still damp hair – she usually left it down unless it needed to be out of the way. It was thick and full, the fiery red color losing no intensity at any interval. Her part was off to the side, making a wavy fringe on the left. Sometimes I wondered what it would feel like to run my fingers through her hair.

Creep.

I shook my head and blinked, trying to focus. I had been staring, but she either didn't catch me or didn't care. She put everything back in her bag, slid her phone into her pocket, and stood up to leave. It was already almost five and I hadn't realized.

"I'll text you when and where to go, okay?" She looked at me, making sure that I registered what she was saying. I nodded, and she smiled as she went out the door. As soon as the latch clicked, I ran to the bathroom and scrubbed my face, looking at myself in the mirror with such disdain and hatred that I couldn't contain it. My skin crawled. I punched the mirror. Pieces shattered around me. My body seemingly moved without my permission, and I picked up one of the shards and closed my fist around it so hard that it drew blood. The pain snapped me back to the moment, and I looked around me, pressure and heat building behind my eyes.

Don't cry, you little bitch.

"Shit," I squeaked.

Why did I do that? Why did I do any of this?

Numb aside from the throbbing cuts on my hand, I cleaned up the bathroom and then lay down on the couch. Picking up my phone, I set an alarm for an hour – I was exhausted and felt like I'd pass out if I tried to get up again without sleeping. Just a little sleep, and I'd be better.

CHAPTER THREE

I woke up to my phone buzzing on the table. Panic rose in my stomach and I got nauseous as I looked at it – I'd slept through the alarm. The buzzing was from Alex texting me that they were leaving the diner she and her date had dinner at. Hastily, I threw on a hoodie and my shoes and ran out the door.

If something happens now, it'll be your fault.

I walked as fast as my legs could carry me to the address she'd given me, getting more and more anxious as time went by.

Approaching the house, I saw that a light was on in the bedroom, but couldn't hear anything and didn't see any other indication of people being home. I paced back and forth a few times, beginning to wonder if she'd given me the wrong address. As I pulled out my phone to double check, I heard Alex's voice echo from inside the house.

"Stop!"

I ran to the door. It wasn't locked, so I barreled inside and rattled the doorknob of the bedroom. This one was locked.

"Stop...please!" Her voice cracked, sounding breathless.

Inhaling sharply, I kicked in the door.

The guy had Alex pinned to the bed, her face red and streaked with tears. Her shirt was ripped at the collar, and her hands were turning a dusky, ashen color from how tightly the guy's hands were wrapped around her wrists.

I darted forward and ripped him off the bed. Slamming him into the wall, his head bounced from the impact. His expression was stunned, as though he hadn't realized I was there up until the moment that I pushed him into the wall. Despite being a fair amount larger than me, he couldn't free himself from my grip. I wanted to hurt him. My brain was charging through options of my next move as I brought my face closer to his. Everything was red.

Alex's sobs snapped me back to reality. I couldn't do this in front of her – I didn't want her to see how aggressive I could get when someone I cared about was threatened. Realizing my hand was around his neck and he was gasping for air, I loosened my grip. Still, I didn't let go.

"If you *ever* come near her again, I'll fucking kill you."

I threw him to the ground. He went into a coughing fit and doubled over, leaning against the wall. Alex was still crying. She had sat up, but otherwise she was rendered motionless by fear. Her face was still red, and my heart dropped from seeing her so upset. I never wanted her to hurt like this. Kneeling down in front of her, I gently touched her arm and nudged her to stand up so that we could leave. I could calm her down later – I didn't want her to be around this guy for another minute. Not only did I want her to never have to see him again, I was also afraid that I might lose control if I so much as glanced in his direction.

Alex shakily stood up, and I let her use me for balance during the walk back to my house. By the time we got back, she'd stopped crying, but hadn't spoken. She still trembled at every step.

I brought her up to my room and wrapped her in a blanket while I dug up some clothes for her to change into. We sat in silence together after I set the clothes next to her on my bed. Her eyes were glassy. It took every ounce of my self-restraint to keep from wrapping my arms around her and kissing her on the forehead. I wanted to hug her, but my prior thought stopped me as I was afraid I'd somehow make it creepy. One creep was enough. Instead, I just pulled my knees up to my chest and sat next to her for what felt like an eternity.

"Can...can I...take a shower?" Her voice was small, like it had come from a mouse.

Her breaths were still irregular, so I helped her up and brought her to the bathroom. Turning the water on and setting the change of clothes on the counter, I glanced over at her again to make sure she was okay before leaving the room. She gave me a weak smile.

Shutting the door to my room, I slid down until I hit the floor and started breathing heavily as I shook and started losing control.

What if I hadn't stopped?

When I'd realized what I was doing, I'd had my hands around the guy's neck just like the figure from my nightmares.

You're just like him. You're going to hurt everyone.

I was late. It was my fault that she was even inside. All of this was my fault.

In one swift motion, I slammed the back of my head into the door. The sensation was jarring, and I could feel my brain bounce against my skull. It made the thoughts stop for a second. My hands were shaking, and I got up to dig through the stash in my top drawer.

I needed it. I'd just go to sleep and then I could stop thinking about how I'd fucked everything up. About how I'd almost let Alex get hurt. How I was almost too late.

The room was spinning, and I hastily pulled the bag, a spoon, lighter, and syringe out of the drawer. I tried to get to my desk, but my legs gave out and I ended up on the floor in front of my bed. Opening the syringe package with my teeth, I got the substance ready and retrieved a dose. My hands shook as I held the syringe up to my arm.

"What the fuck are you doing?!"

The noise made me jump and drop the needle, almost stabbing myself in the leg with it. Alex was standing in my doorway with a horrified look on her face. Her eyes were still slightly red and puffy, but otherwise it seemed like the shower had helped.

Until now.

I hadn't even noticed that the water had turned off, nor did I realize that she'd opened the door while I was in my hectic state. Everything was still spinning, and it felt as though all the air had left the room as I stared up at Alex. She stared back at me in disbelief. Not knowing what to say, I gave up and curled my knees up to my chest and tried to ground myself. My thoughts were still racing, but my head was cloudy. Now it was like trying to see through a fog at the same time that someone was screaming in my ear.

Alex must've also been at a loss for words, as she rarely stayed silent in situations of conflict. She hadn't said a word since her initial remark walking in. Shutting the door behind her, she slowly walked towards me until she was at my bed. Then, she slid down the frame until she was sitting on the floor next to me. I was still frozen, and now my breathing threatened to spiral out of control.

She hates me now.

She knows you're nothing but a piece of shit.

I buried my face in my knees. I couldn't look at her — she'd probably just tell me we couldn't be friends anymore because I was too much trouble. It felt like if I stayed buried, I'd never have to face reality.

Alex nudged closer to me. She ran her hand down my back softly, and it sent shivers down my spine. I still couldn't move. A minute later, I felt her again as she wrapped her arms around me. She rested her chin on my shoulder, and I could smell the shampoo she'd used in her hair. She'd used Mom's — it was a faint floral smell. Her hair usually smelled like vanilla and pomegranates.

Why was she even still here? Why didn't she leave as soon as she'd caught me? We stayed like that for a while, until I finally came out of hiding and leaned my head back against my bed. She sat back a little but kept her hand on my shoulder. I hated that she was the one consoling me right now. She was the one who'd had the shit night. I should be the one making her feel better, not adding to the stress.

"How long have you been doing this?" Her tone was soft. She kept her voice low, and her face wore a look of concern rather than disapproval.

Why wasn't she angry?

She should hate you.

"A year," I mumbled, trying to keep my composure.

"Just...why? Why do this?"

Since she'd already found out the worst, I figured I should at least have the decency to be honest, but I doubted that she would understand.

"It makes things stop."

She squinted at me. I knew she wouldn't get it. Despite that, she still hadn't moved away from me. Maybe she *wanted* to get it? Worth a shot.

"I just...need things to stop sometimes. Everything's always going so fast. So...so loud. All I can hear is screaming in my head and I can't sleep until it stops. I just want it to stop. I can't breathe and then everything spins until I feel like puking."

Alex blinked at me, running her hand down my back. I still wasn't sure if she understood. She looked down at the needle, then picked it up and put the cap back on.

"Where's the rest of it?"

My heart dropped. "No...no. I can't."

"You need help, Liz." She held up the syringe. "This isn't help. This makes things stop in the moment, but everything still comes back, doesn't it?"

I gave her a slight nod, knowing she was right but not wanting to admit it.

"It's just a band-aid. Just like me hopping from guy to guy." She lowered her voice and looked me in the eyes. "I know I don't have much room to talk."

I met her eyes for the first time. Maybe she did understand. Whenever I'd questioned her about the countless dates, she'd always said that it was just for fun. I'd started to believe that, even though I'd always known she was using them to cope with things. It felt surreal to hear her admit that she'd known that as well.

She sighed. "So where's the rest of it?"

I still didn't move. She was right that the drugs were a band-aid. I'd always known that. But it was the only thing I had to stop the bleed. At least a band-aid could hold a tiny part of me together – I was afraid that without it I'd completely fall apart.

She placed her hand back on my shoulder. "Let's make a deal. You stop this, I stop the dates."

Fuck. I was still afraid to give it up, but if it meant that she'd stop risking herself too…I wanted to see her be happy. She probably felt the same way about me.

"We look out for each other. I've got your back, you've got mine." She said softly.

If only she knew what I really wanted.

"…Top dresser drawer," I whispered.

She got up and cleared out the entire drawer. Dropping socks to the ground, she pulled out syringes and lighters galore until it was empty. It hurt to watch, but it was also somewhat relieving to have someone that knew. After she gathered everything up, she put it all in a bag and sat down next to me again.

"I'll drop it in a bin tomorrow."

She grabbed a blanket and wrapped herself up and leaned against me. It felt like sparks shot up the right side of my body with her touch.

"You're scary as fuck when you're like that. How you were tonight."

"I know…I'm sorry." I muttered, hating that she saw me as scary.

You're just like him.

"Don't be. There's a time and a place for scary. That was it. You were right. You've always been right about every douchebag."

"You know I'd never hurt you, right?"

I didn't care about her saying I was right. That was never what I'd wanted. I'd always desperately wanted to be wrong, for her to find someone that treated her right. All I cared about was whether or not she was safe.

She held my hand. "I know. I love you."

The air was gone out of the room again. Everything felt like pins and needles. The hand she was touching felt like it was on fire.

What did she just say?

I was too afraid to say it back. Instead, I turned the focus back on her.

"You know, your shit started when your dad left."

"That's not fair." She wrinkled her nose at me. "You have way more context about me than I do about you."

I snorted. "So I'm right?"

She traced the circles on the blanket with her index finger. "I guess, yeah."

The signs had been pretty obvious, her dad had walked out a couple years ago, and she'd cried for days, weeks. He left a note saying that he just couldn't do it with her mother anymore. He'd addressed it to Alex and made a point to tell her that it wasn't her fault – that he still loved her and wanted to see her, to work out some type of custody agreement so that she could come over regularly. Her mother made sure that didn't happen. She'd demonized him in court and gotten full custody of both Alex and her little sister. He hadn't put up much of a fight though. Something told me that he was afraid of Alex's mother. He didn't want the conflict, so he let them go. That was probably the straw that broke Alex's heart.

"She just doesn't give a shit, all she wants is the perfect daughter to do everything *she* wants. She doesn't care about me being happy." Her voice cracked again.

I didn't want to pry too far, so I kept quiet. She was already exhausted. We both were.

I finally hugged her, a feeling that made my heart flutter. We got in my bed together – normally, she slept in the guest bedroom downstairs, but she was so on edge that I couldn't let her go. I rubbed her back until she fell asleep. Then, I was careful to give her space as I settled in myself. My head was still spinning. I wanted to use so, so badly, but I'd made a promise. I wasn't going to break it the minute her back was turned. It took me hours to fall asleep.

Alex and I woke up late the next morning to the smell of Seth's cooking. It was some kind of teacher development day, so we had the day off. Seth gave us both a smile and set a plate in front of each stool at the kitchen island. He'd made French toast with vanilla and cinnamon, which Alex loved. She could never eat much when she was upset, so if she could get anything down it would be this. I picked at my food. My stomach growled, but I was still nauseated from the night before. Shivers ran up and down my spine. My skin felt clammy. It all felt so surreal. Sometimes I wasn't sure if something actually happened or if it was just another nightmare, but from the bruises on Alex's wrists I knew my memory was telling the truth. She eagerly cut into her toast after pouring some syrup on it – I guess she was feeling a little better.

Seth sat down with his own plate, but not before looking both of us over. His eyes landed on Alex's bruises and my scuffed knuckles. It seemed as though he was too afraid to ask specifics. He knew I'd never hurt her, so his mind must have been racing as to what situation could cause marks on both of us.

"Are you guys okay?" He looked down at his plate as he asked.

I didn't answer, and neither did Alex. Neither of us felt up to talking about it. Thankfully, Seth could gather that fact and chose to change the subject instead.

"You guys slept in the same room last night."

Wait. I change my mind, you can go back to asking if we're okay.

My face flushed red, and my heart skipped a beat as Seth glanced up at me with a sly smile. Did he know?

Shit. Shit, what do I say?

Why was I freaking out so much? Nothing had even happened.

"I didn't want to be alone," Alex stepped in. "Date went bad."

That was all he was getting. It was the truth, and thankfully Alex had said it because I was still mentally panicking about what he had implied with the question. I felt even more nauseated now. Why did this have to be so goddamn stressful? Why couldn't these feelings just leave me alone, let me be at peace? He would know something was up if I didn't eat though, so I pushed around the squares I had cut the toast into to make it seem as though I had eaten more than I did.

Seth gave an understanding nod and knew to stop poking. He grinned when he saw how quickly Alex was devouring her food. More than anything, he loved when people enjoyed his cooking.

"Still your favorite, huh?" he asked, a cheerful tone in his voice.

Alex smiled at him and nodded, her mouth still full of food. I gave up trying to make it look like I was eating – the toast pieces were sufficiently spread around the plate. In reality, I'd probably only eaten half a piece.

Frustration lingered with how nervous I'd gotten when Seth had asked about us being in the same room. It was getting harder and harder to keep a lid on my feelings, and I wanted to stall the inevitable for as long as I could. If Alex found out I liked her, I had no idea how she would react. She never gave me the impression that she'd be disgusted by dating someone who wasn't a guy, but knowing her mom's opinions on the matter made the topic a lot scarier. Even if Alex was okay with it, I doubted she would share my feelings. It would just make things awkward between us. On the off-chance that she did like me, it would just make her life a living hell with her mom. God knows how she'd react. I wasn't going to put her in that position. In my mind, the most likely result of Alex finding out that I was secretly in love with her would be the end of our friendship. I'd rather keep her as my friend than lose her altogether.

Seth raised an eyebrow at me. He'd noticed me space out, and the trick of pushing around the food hadn't fooled him. Alex's plate was completely clean. Had she even licked up the syrup?

I laughed to myself. *What a dork.*

The front door opened, causing me to jump. Shit, I'd forgotten that Alex wasn't supposed to be here.

"Hey, Monica," Seth said, looking at Mom as she dropped her keys on the counter and started rummaging through the cabinet for some tea. He slid a plate to the end of the counter next to her and she smiled and handed him a tea bag, which he started brewing for her as she ate. I cringed as she looked in my and Alex's direction, praying that she'd forgotten about the punishment she'd doled out the night before. She didn't say anything.

Mom had adopted both me and Seth; however she'd taken Seth way earlier than me. He was only seven when he first came to her house, whereas I was twelve. Being a year older than me, that made a six-year difference between us coming into the home. Despite being there so much longer, Seth still called her Monica. He'd explained it to me once – he still remembered his birth mother. I was only four when my mom died, Seth was five. He'd loved his mom dearly *and* witnessed her death. She'd died protecting him from a home invader. No one could replace her in his mind, so the idea of calling Monica "Mom" didn't sit right with him.

Sometimes I was jealous that he at least remembered his mother — all I knew about mine was that she was full-blooded Puerto Rican and her name was Isabelle. Yet my parents named me Elizabeth. How original. I was fairly sure that my father had named me, which made me hate the name even more. Surely my mother wouldn't have named me the English version of her own name? My father was probably too ignorant to realize the connection.

Mom finished off her toast, and Seth handed her the cup of chamomile tea. I glanced over at Alex's wrists again — if mom noticed the bruises she would definitely ask, and wouldn't stop pushing until she got an answer. Neither of us had the energy for that. Alex must have realized that as well, because she muttered "cold" to me and went upstairs to grab a sweatshirt.

Mom thanked Seth for the food and tea, giving him a peck on the forehead. He smiled and took her plate. Just because there was no replacing his birth mom didn't mean that he didn't love Monica like a mother. Flashing a tired smile at me, Mom trudged up the stairs to her bedroom to sleep after her long shift. I guess I really was off the hook. Alex came back down the stairs a minute later, dressed in her clothes from the night before with the exception of one of my t-shirts replacing the shirt that had been torn. She'd also added a hoodie that she wore more often than I did — I'd tried to give it to her so many times, but somehow it kept coming back. She had the bag from last night in her hands, making my heart jump. I tried to suppress my reaction.

"I should go." She ran her hand down my arm, sending the familiar sparks shooting down to my hand. "I told my mom I was staying here last night, but she expected he home an hour ago."

I nodded at her. The idea of her leaving didn't exactly please me – I was still nervous for her. However, it was broad daylight and her house was only one street over. Suggesting that I walk her home might be overkill.

Instead, I called over my shoulder as she went out the door, "text me."

There was a faint "I will" from her as she shut the door.

I scraped my plate into the garbage, avoiding Seth's questioning looks. He was still suspicious about the whole thing.

When I returned to my room, I started digging through the top drawer of my dresser. I came up empty. *Fuck.* She'd completely cleaned it out. I could've easily gone out and gotten more, but I didn't want to break the promise Alex and I had made to each other. Not this soon at the very least. This meant withdrawal. I would've liked to think that I didn't use it often enough for that to happen, but if I was being honest with myself I'd been using it every other day for the past few months. It had turned into an addiction, whether I wanted to admit it or not. I'd never gone off of it once I started using regularly, so I had no idea how bad it would get.

Full of nervous energy, I decided being productive might be the best way to release some of the tension. I turned on some music and laid out a mat on the floor and started doing push-ups. About halfway through my workout routine, there was a knock on my door. *Shit.* My music was too loud, I'd probably woken Mom up. Opening the door, I was instead met with Seth's serious face. He came in and lowered the music, then sat down at the chair in front of my desk. He nodded towards my bed, suggesting I sit down. After shutting the door, I walked over and sat. The nervous energy started boiling up to the surface again – Seth wasn't afraid to grill me alone. He probably just hadn't wanted to do it in front of Alex.

"What the fuck happened last night? I saw her wrists."

I looked down at the flood. "She wasn't lying."

He squinted. "I figured. I mean what did *you* do?"

Cocking my head sideways, my face got hot. "You think I would *ever* hurt her?" My tone was sharp and a bit louder than I'd intended.

He put his hands up before speaking. "No! *I mean*, what did you do to the guy? Is there a body we gotta hide?"

Of course that was what he meant. I was getting defensive. I'd never raised a hand to anyone I cared about, why would he think that? The only time aggression took over was when someone was being threatened – he had a reason to be concerned.

I lowered my voice before speaking again, "I just...threw him around a little. She was crying. I couldn't do more than that in front of her."

He nodded, but didn't seem like he was done.

"You need to tell her."

"What?"

"That you're in love with her."

My heart dropped into my stomach. He did know. God damn it, I knew I was getting worse at hiding it. My thoughts started racing and my hands began to shake. Clammy and nauseated, I didn't know if I was being overtaken by emotions or withdrawal. Probably both.

"Liz, it's hurting you to not tell her, I can see it."

There was no disagreeing with that. Especially in the last few months, I hadn't been able to relax around her at all. Every move I made was calculated with not giving myself away in mind. My vision went blurry as tears began to well up in my eyes. I shut them tight and blinked away the blur. I wasn't going to cry, not in front of anyone.

Seth's voice softened even more than its usual smooth tone. "You know it's okay, right?"

No.

"There's nothing wrong with you."

"That's not what I've been told," I muttered.

I'd had the concept of "you can't like girls" literally beaten into me.

He furrowed his eyebrows at me. "What happened?"

Seth hadn't been in the foster system as long as I had, but he still knew how shitty some foster homes could be. He'd been in at least a few before Mom took him in. I'd been bounced through so many that I lost count. There were enough red flags on my case, people assumed I'd be difficult to deal with. I guess that wasn't wrong.

Avoiding eye contact, I answered him. "I liked a girl in first grade. I didn't even do anything weird – it was Valentine's Day and all I did was make her a card saying she was pretty. She got mad and told me that only boys could give girls Valentines. I didn't understand so when I got home I asked my foster mom what I was supposed to do if I liked a girl. The family had been good to me so far, so I didn't think she'd get mad about me asking a question. She told me never to ask that again, and when the father got home he smacked me around. He told me I was an abomination. I didn't even know what that meant at the time. The next day social services picked me up – the family said they 'didn't want me corrupting their other kids'." I shrugged and finally looked up at Seth. "Ever since then I just kinda assumed I was supposed to be alone."

Seth shook his head and leaned back in the chair. "Some people are fucked up. That's a load of shit. You know it is – you've never even thought twice about me dating guys."

I shrugged. Seth was bisexual, but he had better taste than Alex. I didn't care who he was with as long as they weren't a shitbag.

"You're so understanding with everyone else, why can't you give yourself the same leeway? You deserve to be happy."

"How do you know telling her won't make everything worse?" I pulled my knees up to my chest. I wasn't willing to take a gamble when it meant that I could lose the most important friendship I'd ever had.

Seth ran a hand through his hair and sighed. "It's Alex. she already loves you. She wouldn't drop you over something like that."

"But her mom…"

"You really think she'd share her mom's opinion on anything?"

"No...but I feel like, if it even went anywhere, it would make everything so much worse for her at home."

"So she'd stay here. She practically lives here anyway. Monica loves her, you know she wouldn't care."

I stared down at my floor. Maybe he was right? The idea of telling her still made my heart race, but it seemed slightly more plausible.

"I'll think about it," I muttered.

Seth studied me. He seemed worried – he knew more than anyone how bad I could get. He'd caught me when I first started using and sobered me up before an addiction could fester. He never told anyone because he thought I'd stopped. Knowing he'd definitely tell Mom if he caught me again, I'd gotten a lot more careful after the first time. My nightmares had woken him up many times, and he'd taught me how to patch the walls that I'd punched holes in.

"I get it," he said sympathetically. "I know it's hard. Talk to me if you need anything. I mean it when I say you really do deserve to be happy."

He got up and left the room, closing the door behind him. He was giving me space – I got overwhelmed pretty easily when talking about things I didn't like dealing with. I exhaled sharply and closed my eyes as I leaned against the wall around my bed.

I spent the rest of the day in my room. I tried to watch movies as my shaking became more and more violent and the nausea overcame me. Living next to the trash can, I nursed sips of water in between fits of puking. I hadn't eaten, there was nothing for me to throw up but acid and water. And oh my god, the pain. My stomach cramped so tight I thought it might invert on itself. All my muscles felt like they were on fire. It was a damn good thing I hadn't had to go to school. It was a miserable, awful day. But I got through it. For Alex.

CHAPTER FOUR

I woke up to my phone buzzing on the shelf above my head. It was eight AM on a Saturday, so I cursed as I blindly grabbed for my glasses and dragged the phone down. My anger dissipated as soon as I saw the text was from Jeremy. He'd never text me this early if something wasn't wrong. It had been a few months since we'd met, we'd become pretty good friends, and every once in a while he called me to bail him out of some shitty situations with his mom.

Hey, can you come get me? It's okay if you can't, mom's just on a rampage.

I'm not sure I can get out of the house, but if I have to I can just hide out in my room

Don't worry about it if you can't I'll be okay

I'll be right over

Thanks, sorry you have to keep doing this

He was always extremely apologetic. I'd told him a thousand times that he didn't have to be. I grumbled as I rolled out of bed and got dressed. Not even bothering to brush my hair, I threw it into a ponytail. Putting a jacket on, I left the house – no one else was up. Normally, I would've already been up, but I had been up late the night before texting Alex. I'd gotten *so close* to telling her about my feelings, but wimped out at the last minute like I did every time.

I walked up to the complex where Jeremy lived and trudged up the stairs to his apartment. I was about to knock on the door when I heard a crash inside. It sounded like a plate hitting the wall and shattering.

"Fuck," I muttered.

I'm at the door, what do you want me to do?

She's in the kitchen to the right, I'll sneak into the living room
Can you just open the door and let me out?

Sure

I waited a second, then slowly creaked the door open. It wasn't locked – it was possible Jeremy had already made a run for it and hadn't been successful. That might've been why he texted me. I saw him duck down as another plate went flying across the room in his direction. She'd seen him, there was no sneakily getting out of there now.

"The fuh...the fuck you doin'? Told you to stay in your room." Her speech was slurred. God, this scene was so familiar.

She hadn't noticed that the door was ajar enough for me to be able to see in. Jeremy glanced in my direction but tried not to draw attention to me. He was shaking – he was used to a certain degree of brutality from his mother, but she wasn't usually throwing things. Not knowing what to expect probably made him more anxious. Another plate flew into the living room and shattered when it collided with a bookshelf.

"Get the...the fuck over here."

No.

I wasn't going to watch this happen. Throwing the door open, I rushed inside and got in front of Jeremy. I stood face to face with his mother. She was a mess. Her shirt was covered in stains and looked as though she hadn't changed it in a couple days. There were bottles and cans all over the kitchen, and she wobbled as she took a step forward. She wasn't too intoxicated to put up a fight, but it would be easier for me to evade flying objects if she couldn't see straight to aim.

"The fuck are you?"

Jeremy stood behind me, frozen. He didn't want to leave without me, but I knew he also desperately wanted out of the situation.

I didn't even address his mother. I didn't care about her. "Let's go." Glancing behind me, I gestured towards the door.

"Don't even think about it, you little shit." She picked up another plate.

A push, and Jeremy was out the door. I was right behind him and turned to grab the knob. A plate shattered on the wall right next to my head. The noise echoed in my ears as I slammed the door.

A liquor bottle hit the wall and smashed a few inches away from me. I was small, so the shards rained down around me like a summer storm.

"You been gettin' into my food again?" A man's voice angrily yelled at me. Quivering, I stared up at him.

Why can't I move?

Feeling a pain in my stomach, I doubled over while still trying to watch the man. I was so hungry. All I ever got were scraps, like a dog. The man yanked his belt out of its worn loops and stood over me. He towered over me. There was nothing I could do. I lay down on the floor and covered my head. Some of the glass shards pressed into my arms, but it was nothing compared to the searing pain of the belt hitting my exposed legs. They felt like they were on fire.

"Liz?" Jeremy's voice was tentative.

He reached out to touch my shoulder, but quickly pulled his hand away as I flinched.

"Fuck," I muttered.

He'd managed to pull me out of it, but my legs still stung with heat. I still had scars from that day. I almost always wore long pants to cover them up, even in the summer, regardless of the temperature. Most people didn't even know I had them.

"I...I'm sorry." Tears welled up in his eyes.

He always felt so bad about asking me to help. I'd never told him about my past, but it was easy to tell I got thrown into flashbacks when confronting his mother. "It takes one to know one" rang incredibly true in this case.

There was more crashing and yelling inside the apartment, but thankfully it didn't seem as if the woman was going to follow us. If she had planned on it, she would've already been at the door. I turned around and glanced at Jeremy before starting down the stairs.

"Let's go."

Everything felt so blurry as we walked through the city back to my house. I was walking through fog. Nothing was real. I don't remember most of the walk, it seemed like we were just suddenly back at my house with me unlocking the door. We went up to my room, and I went straight for my top dresser drawer. The stash didn't contain anything hard anymore – just a little bit of weed. I took out the supplies and started rolling a blunt. It wouldn't help a ton, but it might take the edge off.

Jeremy spun slowly in my desk chair, stopping to watch me. "Liz…"

"Don't." It was misdirected, I wasn't mad at him.

"I mean just…you've gotta talk about this shit with someone. You zone and then you're not okay when you come back."

"Yeah? Who do you talk to?" My tone cut like a razor.

He sighed. "You."

"Exactly." I was his confidant, he wasn't going to be mine. I wouldn't put that weight on him.

"That doesn't mean you can't talk to me. Or Alex. Hell, even Monica. Just, someone. I should know keeping all that shit under wraps just gets too hard. I don't know how I did it before we met."

I finished rolling the blunt and lit it, inhaling deeply before letting out the smoke. Handing the blunt over to him, I rolled my eyes.

"I've got it under control." I didn't. But everyone needed to believe that I did.

He looked away from me as he took in a drag. He made a face, however quickly. He'd done his best for me to not see, but

I'd caught it.

"What?"

"Nothing." He muttered, handing me back the blunt.

Furrowing my eyebrows, my tone grew sharper. "What?"

"You're not going to like it."

"Shoot." I took another puff.

"You...you really don't. You drink like crazy half the time, and you were doing harder shit up until Alex caught you. You lash out at the first person to cross you. Other times you seem like you're not even there." His words cut into me, hitting the heart of everything I tried to hide.

Okay, now maybe I was a little mad at him. "Fuck off."

"Told you you wouldn't like it. I'm only saying it because I care. You can't keep going like this forever."

"It's worked well enough for ten years." I waved him off while passing the blunt over again.

There was no rebuttal. He wouldn't win this fight with me.

I got up, grabbing my skateboard. "C'mon, let's go."

We made our way to the skate park – I needed to do something to clear my head. The weed hadn't helped much. The fog was back and I felt like I was walking through a dream, like nothing around me was actually happening. Since Alex had told Jeremy about the deal we'd made a few months ago, she'd asked him to keep an eye on me when we were skating. She knew it would be easy for me to slip and buy something while I was at the park. At least she understood that I still needed to skate, especially if I was going to stay off the drugs. Jeremy had a pretty timid personality, but he had enough backbone to stand up to me when needed. If he so much as caught me glancing around to find a dealer he'd shoot me a look that could kill. Taking him with me right now was kind of a relief – I was in a bad state of mind where I'd be more likely to make the wrong choice. He could help curb it before something happened. Somehow, I'd managed to stay clean since the night that Alex caught me, and I didn't want to ruin everything.

When we got to the park, Alex was standing near the entrance. Her eyes darted back and forth across the environment and then back down at her phone. She stopped when she saw me and Jeremy. Narrowing her eyes, she glared at me.

What did I do now?

"Where were you?" Her tone was sharp.

"What?" I didn't have a clue what she was talking about. Squinting, I tried to figure out what it was that made her angry.

"Lunch?"

Oh, shit. I was supposed to meet her for lunch. *Wait, what time is it?*

I pulled out my phone and looked down at the screen. Besides a few texts and a missed call from Alex, the display said one PM. I'd lost *two hours?* Jeremy and I had stopped back at my house, but I'd gotten to his house at nine, and there was no way we'd spent more than two hours at my house. That still left eleven AM through one PM unaccounted for. Were we really at my house that whole time? I hated this fog.

Dazed, I looked back up at Alex. "I'm sorry."

Her face softened. She could tell I hadn't meant to ditch her. She sighed, putting her phone back in her pocket.

"You look pale." She touched my face.

Goddamn sparks.

I shrugged. Inviting her to stay, Jeremy and I entered the park. Alex never really seemed fond of the place, which was fair. She didn't really have an interest in skating, and there were plenty of skeevy guys around to bother her. She had bad taste, but at the very least she had some standards. I'd be there like a rabid dog to chase them off. In broad daylight she didn't seem to mind the place too much. On a Saturday afternoon there were a couple families around, rather than the usual crowd.

Jeremy and I skated for a couple hours. Gradually, the families started to leave and the usual people started coming in. Alex began to squirm. She knew I wouldn't let anything happen to her, but I think that might've been what she was afraid of. I could definitely go too far defending her. Gesturing to Jeremy, I stopped and walked up to the bench where Alex was sitting. She flashed me a half smile.

"Wanna go?"

"Please," she said, scanning the park and then looking back at me.

I felt a little better, but there was still a dull fog around everything. We'd go home and watch a movie or something, the three of us. Forget about all the shit that went on. We had to walk by a couple guys near the entrance. Of course, as we walked by they both had to comment.

"The redhead's pretty damn hot." One said to the other.

"Eh." The other kid waved his hand. "I'd tap the Spanish chick all day."

Spinning around on my heels, my rage consumed me. Alex caught my arm before I could do anything.

"Liz, don't."

I tried to focus. She was right, it wasn't worth it. Just a couple hecklers with nothing better to do. We continued walking by them and I tried to ignore their presence.

Then it happened. The guy that had commented on me reached out and slapped my butt.

Fuck no.

I ripped away from Alex's grip and flew into the kid's face. As I threw him against the fence, he tried to stop himself from falling. The other kid ran away. I took another step and moved my face in closer, just inches from his.

"You fuckin' touch me?"

The kid looked as though he wasn't sure if he should make another snarky comment or back down. He wasn't nearly as scared as he should've been.

"Yeah, babe, didn't you like it?"

Wrong choice.

Everything went red. I threw him to the ground and got down on top of him. I repeatedly laid my fist into his face. There was faint yelling in the background, but my ears were ringing, I couldn't hear what was being said. Slamming the kid's head into the pavement, I kept punching. Everything was moving so quickly and I couldn't stop. Blood splattered onto my face and hands.

A firm grip yanked me off the kid and pinned me to the ground. The impact knocked the wind out of me. Panicking, my first instinct was to fight back. I kicked my legs out and struggled against the man's grip. Screaming, my thoughts started racing through every possibility of what he would do to me. I kept thrashing underneath him, and he leaned his weight onto my shoulders to keep me down. It was hard to breathe, and I kept scraping my face on the pavement. Cold metal tightened around my wrists behind my back.

I realized that the man on top of me was a cop. I wasn't sure if I was better or worse off because of that. Would he shoot me?

My body kept fighting back even though my brain was screaming to stop, and I gasped for air as the man put more and more weight on my back.

"Fuckin' stop!" the man yelled at me.

I wanted to, but I couldn't. Slamming my head into the pavement, my body kept doing everything it could to get out from under him until it was exhausted. I kept hitting my head on the pavement until blood started to drip from my forehead.

You deserve to die.

"Tucker!" A woman's voice yelled as sirens blared, coming closer to us.

At the sound of the woman's voice, the man loosened his grip on me and took his weight off of my back. I still couldn't breathe. Why couldn't I breathe? I gasped for air as everything around me spun. I couldn't tell if the vertigo was from lack of oxygen or from slamming my head into the pavement. My breathing remained erratic, and I started choking on my own spit. What was happening? I couldn't control anything. Everything was so fast. I could hear voices around me but couldn't understand what they were saying. There was crying in the background. Was that Alex? I still couldn't focus and the thought left my head as quickly as it had come. My mind wouldn't stop racing.

Then, I felt a soft touch on my shoulder. I still couldn't see straight, but the familiar spark told me who it was. She turned me on my side. I was still handcuffed, but it was easier to breathe than when I was on my stomach. My ears were still ringing and my breath still wouldn't stay in my lungs. She sat down next to me and kept stroking my shoulder until, finally, my breathing began to slow.

"Liz…" Her voice cracked.

You did it this time. Fucked everything up for good.

I could faintly understand the voices around me now, over the shrill noise of my ears.

The woman who had yelled was also a cop. She was the polar opposite to her partner. He was a young-looking and muscular white guy who must've been at least 6'5". The woman had dark skin, was much shorter, and had a much calmer air about her. Her face still said she wouldn't take shit from anyone, but her demeanor suggested she at least had a scrap of humanity. She was probably the one who had let Alex come over to me. The man had seemed content to lean into my back until I passed out. The sirens I'd heard weren't more police, but an ambulance for the kid I'd unleashed on.

Fuck. Fuck, fuck! Did I kill him? Am I a murderer now?

I was still unable to talk, but the woman came over and sat me up. Her grip was firm but gentle. Everything spun more when I was upright, and blood dripped down my face from my forehead. This place looked like it was a murder scene. It probably was. I was going to prison forever. Everyone always said that's where I'd end up.

Slowly, the cop helped me up and led me over to the car. She supported my weight a lot more than I'd expected. I could barely stand up and didn't realize how much I was leaning on her. She sat me down in the car and slammed the door shut, talking to her partner. She then got in the driver's seat and he sulked into the passenger side. She was the one in charge.

I was silent the whole way to the police station. They didn't ask me any questions during the car ride. They wouldn't have gotten an answer anyway. I still couldn't process what was happening. Walking me into the station, they sat me in a room with a table. They linked the handcuffs in front of me to a loop on the table so I couldn't leave. Then, they both exited. I was alone.

CHAPTER FIVE

A faint smell of coffee filled the room, a lone sense of humanity in an otherwise cold and industrial-looking place. The place didn't look like the police interrogation rooms you'd see on television – the only consistent piece was the cold metal table in the middle. Otherwise, it was much smaller. It was dingy and painted with a sad-looking off-white color. There was no one-way mirror. In fact, there were no windows at all. The door didn't even have one. There was a small camera up in the corner of the room though – probably a cheaper alternative.

I drew circles on the table with my index finger, the chain of the handcuffs clinking against the surface. My head hurt so bad. I couldn't think. My eyes wouldn't focus. None of this felt real – not the chair I was sitting on, not even the room which I'd been staring at for at least twenty minutes at this point. For once, my mind wasn't racing – it was the complete opposite. It was as though someone had just hit an "off" switch, and all my functioning had gone with it. The fog was there, but there was nothing to see beyond it. Nothing but empty space. I still wanted to slam my head against the table, but this time it wasn't to stop the thoughts. It was because I felt like I deserved it – I had earned the punishment. I deserved everything that had ever happened to me.

I jumped as the hinges on the door squeaked, and the woman from earlier stepped in. She didn't look angry – she was the most composed-looking person I'd ever seen. She wasn't devoid of emotion – her slightly upturned eyebrows and faint smile alluded to her concern. She should've been screaming at me, shouldn't she?

Pulling out the chair across from me, she spoke for the first time. "Hello, Elizabeth." Her voice was low and soft like it had been before. How can someone always be that calm? She continued, "My name's Akilah." She had a faint accent that I couldn't place.

She knew my name, and judging by the amount of time I'd been sitting alone in the room, she'd been able to read my case record. I didn't know where she was going to go with this, or to what degree I'd fucked myself over. My record wasn't exactly clean, but it also wasn't severe enough to get me locked up forever. At least, I didn't think so. I glanced up at her face to acknowledge that she'd spoken, then mustered up the courage to ask a question.

"Did I kill him?" My voice cracked.

The woman leaned back in her chair, folding her hands into one another. "No, hon. He's got a broken nose and a fractured cheekbone, but that's all."

I nodded, staring at the table.

At least I'm not a murderer.

"His record isn't clean either – his parents have already said that they don't want to press charges."

What the fuck?

"Did he do anything to you?"

He had a record. Of what? I furrowed my eyebrows. The advances he'd made towards me were ones that I'd grown to expect from people – I'd never seen anyone get in trouble for it. Had he done worse before?

Glancing back up at Akilah, I realized I'd been silent for too long. How was she so patient?

"He grabbed my a—" I stopped myself. Could you get in trouble for swearing in front of a cop? I didn't know. "...He spanked me."

She huffed. "Well, what a dick."

What?

This didn't seem like how this was supposed to go at all. Was I being set up for something?

"You know that doesn't mean what you did was okay, yes? There's self-defense and then there's...well...full-on assault."

I nodded. The woman reached over, unlocked the handcuffs.

"Now, I can't release you until your guardian is here since you're a minor. But you're no longer under arrest."

I pulled my knees up to my chest while sitting in the chair. As I wrapped my arms around my legs, I rested my chin on top of my knees. Why was she still talking to me? Why didn't they just throw me in a cell until Mom came?

Oh god, Mom. She'll be furious. I fucked up real bad this time. Was there a way for her to un-adopt me? If there was, she'd probably do it. I'd always been too much trouble. For everyone.

"Hon…" Akilah's voice brought me back to reality. "I want to talk to you about something else. You're not obligated to talk to me about it, but I want you to hear me out."

I made eye contact, waiting for her to go on.

"You probably guessed that I had a look at your record while you were in here."

Oh god, where is she going with this?

"I see a lot of typical behaviors of foster kids who've had it tough – unwillingness to communicate with adults, difficulty in school, various homes that gave you up for 'undesirable behaviors'. But...there's a couple things that stick out."

Oh fuck no...

"The first one being the first home you had an extended stay in – you where there for a year, but then they abruptly turned you back over to foster care. They said you'd pulled a knife on the father? You were nine at the time, that's a pretty drastic behavior. A red flag, if you will."

I'm not talking about this. She can lock me away forever first.

"Something happened there, didn't it?"

No. No no no.

My face started burning up and tears tried to force their way to the surface. I dug my fingernails into my jeans until my knuckles turned white. My eyes lost focus.

Stop...stop it.

"This is the kind of stuff you have to deal with, get out in the open, if things are going to get any better, you know? You can't just bottle everything up, that's how things like today happen."

No reaction.

She offered me a faint smile. Leaning forward and pressing her hands against the metal of the table, she lowered her voice even more. "As concerning as that first point is, it's the second one I'm more worried about."

Please stop.

"Before you came to your current home, you were in a group home, yes?"

My heart started racing.

"There's a hospital stay on record for three days after you entered the group home. The intake states an apparent overdose of over-the-counter painkillers. The statement the police took said one of the aids had accidentally left the bottle on the counter."

The tears were trying to force their way out again. I wouldn't let them.

"A kid as street smart as you knows the difference between ibuprofen and candy, even as a twelve-year-old."

I started grinding my teeth. My jaw wouldn't unclench, and my chest felt so tight I thought I might never breathe again.

"Hon...you need help. You can't keep going on like this. You're either going to land yourself in prison or die from reckless, desperate choices."

There they were again, the same words that Alex had said to me. "You need help."

No one can help you. You're too broken.

"I'm going to suggest some therapists and programs to your guardian when she arrives. I can't make you do anything, but I see a lot of kids like you go down the wrong path. I don't want to see you hurt yourself or anyone else."

She won't even want me when she gets here. She'll jump at the chance to send me away.

"Do you remember what happened when we arrested you?"

I shrugged, glad that she'd dropped the prior line of questioning. She'd figured out more skimming through my file than anyone ever had, I thought she'd try and pry everything out of me.

"You had trouble breathing, weren't able to respond, and you were shaking. I don't know if you've ever had that happen before, but those are all classic signs of a panic attack."

It had happened before. More than once.

"You've got too much in your head to handle, kiddo. It's not bad to ask for help. In fact, it takes a lot of courage."

I won't make other people deal with my problems. That's selfish.

A knock on the door, and Akilah opened it and stepped into the hallway. A few minutes later, Mom took a step inside the doorway, a stack of papers and brochures in hand.

"Let's go." Her voice was harsh. I knew she'd be angry with me.

I got up and followed her without a word, staring at the ground the whole time. We got to the car, and I sank into the passenger's seat, avoiding eye contact. Mom pulled out of the parking lot and we drove in silence for a few minutes.

Eventually, she broke the quiet.

"What are we going to do with you?" The harsh tone had left her voice – she sounded more defeated than anything.

I was a disappointment, I'd always fuck things up.

Staring at my hands, I leaned against the car door. There was dried blood all over me, and my head was still pounding.

You're such a piece of shit.

An apology wouldn't mean anything right now, so I didn't even bother. It seemed as though it would be more insulting than anything.

"The policewoman suggested getting you into therapy, maybe even a program."

I knew she'd send me away.

"You've always resisted the idea, I know – but I think she's right. I don't think I can give you a choice this time, Liz. This shit isn't okay."

I pulled my knees up to my chest and buried my face, covering the back of my head with my hands. Everything needed to stop. I didn't need another person to tell me how bad I'd fucked everything up, I already knew that.

Nothing's going to help.

Mom let out a sigh.

She's giving up on you.

Good! No one should have to deal with me.

The rest of the ride was silent. I didn't pick my head up until I felt the car stop and heard her shift it into park. We got out of the car and went inside, and I went straight up to my room. Seth gave Mom a questioning look, but I avoided eye contact with him and didn't bother to check Mom's reaction – I already knew how she felt. I didn't care if she told him.

He already knows what a fuck up you are.

Shutting my door softly, I leaned back against it and slid to the ground. Tears tried to force their way out of my eyes again, but I refused. My vision was blurry as I looked up at the ceiling. The room was dark, the sun had long since gone down. Everything felt numb, but hurt at the same time. How does that even work? I wanted to scream.

Everyone would be better off if you were dead.

I got up and went to the bathroom to wash some of the blood off. Red stained the water as I cleaned the blood from my hands. His blood. I dabbed a washcloth at the blood on my head. My blood. Looking in the mirror, my reflection painted a picture of defeat. My eyes bloodshot, a gash in my head, dark circles under my eyes. I hated every part of me. I put my hand over the mirror to avoid punching this one like I'd done with the one downstairs. I wondered if anyone had noticed that yet. It was a small issue in comparison with the current ones, I guess it didn't really matter.

Going back to my room, I dug through my top dresser

drawer as I had in the past. I still kept my money there. Pulling out a wad of cash, I stuffed it in my pocket. My clothes were still splattered with dried blood, but I didn't care. I opened my window screen, dropped down onto the roof, and then the ground. Starting down the street, I didn't look back. It would be a while before they realized I was gone. Mom had work soon, and Seth usually left me alone – if anything he wouldn't try to check in with me until Mom left for the night.

I won't be their problem anymore.

I walked until I reached the familiar skate park. It was fairly empty now, but the shady characters always lurked in the shadows. Walking up to Tony, I made eye contact and then flashed some money.

I'm sorry Alex. It'll only be this once.

Tony looked at me and chuckled, less secretive now that he had the cover of darkness.

"Hey!" he said, "long time no see."

I shrugged. He acted like we were friends. Like we weren't just using each other as a means to an end.

"You want your usual? I still remember."

"More." My tone was gruff.

"Alright."

He handed me a larger bag than usual and took the cash. He also slipped a still-packaged syringe into my hand.

"On the house."

It was a good thing; I didn't have any left. I turned away without saying a word. He didn't care about me any more than I cared about him – he was just trying to keep me coming back.

"Hey, Liz!" he yelled after me.

I turned around, still only a few feet away from him.

"Be careful, yeah? If it's been a while you'll have less of a tolerance. You've always been a good customer, I'd hate to lose you like that."

Turning back on my heels, I huffed. What an ass. He didn't give a shit about me, all he cared about was the money. It was the pretend concern for my well-being that bugged me. Why not just sell to me and call it a day?

My mind was foggy and blank at the same time. It was as though I wasn't in my body, the actions were just carrying themselves out without me even trying. I trudged towards the back of the skate park, passing the blood stain on the pavement from earlier.

Everything's your fault.

Once I reached the very back of the park, I scaled the fence and dropped down to the other side. It was a grungy alleyway with a dumpster sitting against the fence.

Exactly where I belong.

Sliding to the ground opposite of the dumpster, I pulled out my phone. I stared at the screen for a long time with it open on a conversation with Alex. She'd sent me a few texts while I'd been at the police station.

We've gotta talk. This shit is too much.
Hey, are you okay?
Text me.

Between bouts of spacing out while staring at Alex's messages, I sent Seth a text.

Jeremy's mom's been beating the shit out of him
Either take care of him or tell someone, I don't care which

Eventually, I found the right words for Alex. I sent the message off, then threw my phone as far as I could. It shattered as it landed in the street, cars running it over shortly after. Then, I pulled out the bag and the syringe. All I could hear were Alex's sobs as the cop had ripped me off the kid.

This is best for everyone. You won't be able to hurt people anymore. You can't cause anyone trouble if you're dead. You're nothing but an inconvenience to anyone you meet — you just make things harder for everyone. You ruin everything. You never deserved to be alive in the first place.

I couldn't stop the tears this time. My face grew hotter and hotter as I tried and failed to force back the sobs that overcame me. Shakily, I pulled out the syringe and the bag and stared at them for what felt like forever.

Just fucking do it. Everyone will be happier.

Pulling back on the syringe, I filled it to the top after melting down the powder in a spoon I'd tossed in my pocket. I held up my arm. My hand shook, but it didn't matter.

Don't be selfish. Stop being a fucking wuss. Do everyone a favor.

I plunged the needle into my arm and pushed all of the liquid in. Every last drop. I threw the needle and other items away. My body began to shake as I felt colder. Leaning back against the wall, I closed my eyes as the world around me grew more and more faint.

CHAPTER SIX

You're the best thing that ever happened to me. I want you to know that none of this is your fault, you never did anything to deserve all the grief I've brought you.

There's a few things I need to tell you, because it's not fair for me to keep them from you anymore.

I love you.

I never said it back regardless of how many times you said it to me. I'm just shit at this kind of thing and it comes so easily to you. I love you as my best friend, one of the first people to ever show me real kindness. You make me feel safe in ways I never thought I'd trust anyone.

But, I love you as more than a friend too. I was afraid to tell you because I didn't want to lose you altogether, but in retrospect I have no idea why I thought you'd be so fickle. You'd never do that and I know it. It was my own insecurities that kept me from telling you. You're the most beautiful person I've ever known, inside and out. The way your lips curl at the edges when you grin always made my heart flutter, and every time you touched me it was like electricity shooting into my skin. I never told you much about my life before I came to stay with Monica, and it always seemed like you took that pretty personally. It wasn't your fault. It wasn't that I didn't trust you. I had two reasons — first, that I didn't want to dump my problems on you. Second, saying things out loud made them real.

Fuck it, though. They're real anyway. It's only fair that I answer the one question that came up so many times — why do I get so aggressive when other people get hurt?

The answer is pretty simple, and I should've given it to you a long time ago. It's because I know what it feels like to be hurt by people. I don't want anyone else to have to experience that, especially people I really care about. If you hadn't still been in the room, I probably would've killed the guy that tried to force himself on you. I almost lost control that day, because the thought of you even coming close to that experience broke my heart, and I wanted to hurt anyone that would try to do that to you. My anger hurt the people I cared about too though, no matter how hard I tried.

Today I made you cry because I almost killed someone, and you still came to try and help me. You were always there for me when I needed it, no matter how hard it was. I'm not good enough for you — I don't deserve you.

Please, don't blame yourself for anything. I know you do that when things go wrong and it's never true. You're amazing. You'll have a great life, just keep your head up and don't listen to a damn word your mother says. I hope you get to see your dad again.

I love you.

I blinked back tears, staring at my phone screen. I didn't know how to react. There was so much in front of me. So many questions ran through my mind. Why was she telling me this now? How hadn't I seen her crush before? Why did she keep telling me not to blame myself?

My heart dropped as the thought flashed into my mind: this was a goodbye. It sounded so final, so absolute. At no point was she looking for a response from me. She'd written about the future like she wouldn't be there to see it. I started to panic, and halfway through a text reply I closed it and called instead.

There was no answer; the phone didn't even ring. I got an automated voice telling me that the number I'd called was out of service. My heart started to race and I hung up, dialing Seth's number instead.

"What's up?" he asked.

"Is Liz home?" My voice was frantic as my heart kept jumping into my throat with each beat.

"She went up to her room last I saw. Why aren't you calling her?"

"I did. The phone didn't even ring."

"Weird..." He trailed off, seemingly distracted by something else.

"Please just check." My tone sharpened as I started to lose my patience. There wasn't time for this. Why wasn't he more worried? Sometimes it seemed like he was oblivious to the world around him.

He was silent for a minute, but I could hear him walking up the steps. I started to pace my room, getting more and more anxious. I heard him call Liz's name a few times, then put the phone back up to his ear, slightly more out of breath.

"She's not here, it looks like she went out the window."

I got lightheaded, and my whole body started to tingle as though all the blood were just draining out straight through my feet.

"Did she text you?"

"Hang on." He probably had to look. He wasn't great about checking his phone. "Yeah...Jeremy's mom is abusive?"

"Fuck, she'd never tell anyone that unless..."

I sprang up and put shoes on, running out the door and ignoring my mom yelling after me. I'd deal with her later, this was more important.

"What?" Seth's tone had a slight edge to it now.

I realized I hadn't finished my thought out loud. "Unless she wasn't going to be here to protect him anymore."

"I'll call Monica." He finally understood.

"I'm checking the park."

I hung up, shoving my phone in my pocket as I began to sprint down the street towards the skate park. I wasn't fond of that place during the day and was especially nervous to be there at night. The panic from Liz's message overtook the anxiety I felt for myself. I recognized a figure standing in the shadows. I didn't even care that normally I was terrified of him.

"Has Liz been by here?" I asked, trying to hide the panic in my voice.

"Who wants to know?"

What a fucking ass. Getting in his face, I yelled, "I do! Fucking tell me which way she went!"

He threw his hands up. "God damn, calm down spitfire. She headed towards the back of the park."

I didn't even glance back at him as I ran towards the back of the park where it connected with an alleyway, only a chain link fence between them. I squinted in the dark as I put my hands up to the fence. There was a person sitting in the alley, but I couldn't make out any defining features. Using all my strength, I tried to climb the fence. I fell to the ground after attempting to pick up my second foot. How the fuck did she make this look so easy when she did it? Glancing around, I found a break in the fence the next alleyway over. I ran and squeezed through it, scraping my arm on the metal. Looping around, I got to the right alley and knelt down in front of the person I'd seen to get a good look.

It was Liz. She was pale, and there was spit running down the sides of her mouth. Her lips and fingertips were a dusky blue.

"Liz!" I screamed, shaking her in an attempt to wake her up.

Her body ragdolled as I let go. She was so cold. Trembling as I pulled out my phone, I dialed 911. I tried my best to keep my composure long enough to explain where we were and how I'd found her. I dropped my phone as soon as the operator told me that an ambulance was on the way, and scooted closer to Liz. When I was younger, I'd taken a junior lifeguarding course, so I knew how to check vital signs. I placed two fingers against her neck, trying to find a pulse. It took a minute, but I was able to find an extremely faint beat. Not good, but better than nothing. While checking her pulse I watched for breathing. Her breaths were shallow and erratic. There was a wheeze each time she inhaled. Positioning myself next to her, I lowered her down onto her side. They'd taught us that it was easier for people to breathe on their side, and that it would help keep airways clear. Judging by the amount of spit running down her face, she'd definitely been choking.

Sirens blared as an ambulance approached, and I ran to the end of the alley to wave them down. They pulled over and a couple EMTs jumped out the back of the truck as I ran back to Liz. I tried to stand back as they did a quick exam of the scene and seamlessly moved her onto a stretcher. It was so hard to not get in the way. I wanted to let them do their job because I knew I couldn't help save her at this point, but I also didn't want to leave her.

One of the EMTs glanced back at me and nodded his head towards the ambulance. "Coming?"

I ran behind them and they gestured for me to get in the front. I'd always seen people ride in the back with the person, so I was more nervous to be in the front. Did they need the extra room because she was in such bad shape? Were they afraid of her dying in front of me? Anxiously, I peered through the window separating me from the back of the ambulance. They'd put an oxygen mask on her, and one of the EMTs looked up at the front, straight at me.

"Do you know what she took?"

"P-probably heroin." I shuddered, afraid of being wrong, but also fairly certain that I wasn't. She'd broken our promise, but I didn't care about that now. I just wanted her to be okay.

The woman nodded and called to another EMT in the back. They gave Liz an injection of something, I assumed to counteract the drug. Afterwards, they seemed to be monitoring vital signs. The driver gave me an empathetic smile as I shifted in the seat, trying to see everything that was going on.

Someone called, "No pulse."

My heart dropped and there was organized chaos of EMTs assigning CPR roles to each other in the back. One immediately started chest compressions, and I flinched each time she pressed into Liz's chest. It was necessary for any kind of chance at her survival, but I also knew it wasn't uncommon for ribs to be broken during CPR. Gasping, I realized that I'd been holding my breath. The ambulance pulled into the emergency bay at the hospital where Monica worked, and I watched as they pulled the stretcher out of the back, an EMT kneeling over Liz on it to keep the chest compressions going. The group ran in through the doors and down a hallway until I couldn't see them anymore. I opened the door and tried to hop out, but my legs gave out and I hit the ground, skinning my knees on the pavement.

The adrenaline of trying to get her help was starting to wear off now that I'd done everything I could. Everything started spinning, and I retched, unable to stop myself from puking next to the truck. The ambulance driver came around the side and held back my hair, then supported me as I leaned back. I wiped my mouth and spit on the ground, trying to get rid of the acidic taste.

"You did good, kid," the driver said.

His voice had a calm, soothing tone to it, as if this were just an everyday part of his job. Well, I guess it was. He helped me up and brought me into the lobby of the hospital where Monica rushed over to me.

"I've got her," she said, nodding at the man and giving him a weak smile.

As soon as he left, I completely lost my composure. I fell into Monica, sobbing uncontrollably. She held me tightly and waited a few minutes, likely hoping I'd be able to stop. I couldn't. She guided me to a small exam room and sat me down in one of the chairs. I think she was looking for work to do to try and keep herself composed. She started checking me over. She cleaned the scratches on my arm from the fence as well as the scrapes on my knees. All the marks were fairly superficial, so she left them open rather than completely dressing them. She then grabbed me a blanket and wrapped me in it, handing me a cup of water a minute later. I still couldn't stop crying. My entire body shook, and Monica kept her hand on my back.

It was in her nature to help people. I think she did it to keep busy a lot of the time. If she hadn't been tending to me right now, she'd probably be as much of a mess as I was. She started talking to me, but I didn't really understand what she was saying between my sobs. Eventually, I was able to slow down and calm myself a little. It had been over an hour. We both looked up as a nurse walked into the room and said something to Monica. I still couldn't really make out what people were saying.

After the nurse left, Monica helped me out of the chair and guided me down the hallway to a room. She opened the door and I saw Liz, unconscious in a bed with a tube down her throat to help her breathe. I could feel the tears forcing their way back into my eyes, but I wasn't sobbing anymore. I didn't have the energy to. Monica pushed a couple chairs together next to the bed, then laid down a pillow and gave me another blanket. I lay down in the little makeshift cot, halfway leaning on the bed to stare at Liz.

Monica said something that I didn't hear again, but then knelt down next to me and put her hand on my shoulder to make sure I really understood. I squinted and tried my best to focus on what she was saying.

"She's going to be okay. You saved her life."

A wave of relief washed over me, and I looked back over at Liz. I reached out for her hand and held it tightly. Monica said she'd be okay. That was the physical assessment. How would she be when she woke up? I was so overwhelmed I couldn't even try to process everything that happened. Monica got up and left the room, her eyes glassy. I think she was leaving so that I didn't see her break down too. After she left, I held onto Liz's hand and fell asleep, exhausted.

I woke up late the next morning. The breathing tube down Liz's throat had been replaced with a thin tube underneath her nose that supplied oxygen. That meant she was breathing on her own again. Sitting up in the chair, I looked towards the wall to see Seth fidgeting in the chair, playing games on his phone. There was a lunch pack next to him. He hated hospitals. I don't know what it was, but he always looked like a deer in the headlights the second he was inside any kind of medical facility.

He glanced up and realized that I was awake. "Hey." He dug some food out of the lunch bag. "Hungry at all?"

I nodded. I was and I wasn't at the same time, but my stomach won out with its protesting growls. He handed me a thermos and a grilled cheese wrapped in plastic. They were both still warm. Inside the thermos, there was some creamy tomato basil soup. Smiling at Seth, I unwrapped the sandwich and dipped it in the soup before taking a bite. It was a warm comfort that helped settle my nerves a little. After finishing off the food, I handed the thermos back to him and pulled out my phone.

It was time to try and wrap my brain around the message that Liz had sent me. Before I could even get to my messages, my phone blew up with texts from my mom demanding that I come home and threatening me with how much trouble I'd be in. She wasn't even looking for an explanation, she just wanted to scream at me. I sent a message back telling her what had happened, and that I wasn't coming home right now. Then, I turned off notifications from her. I didn't care what she had to say right now. She'd scream at me later regardless.

I opened Liz's message and read it over and over, five or six times. There was just so much. I thought back to all the times I'd questioned her as to why she didn't date. I felt oblivious for not realizing it sooner. All the times I'd felt her squirm when I reached out for her in a hug. Did she feel like hugging me back would be taking advantage of me because I didn't know? Or was she afraid that I'd figure it out if she showed any affection at all? Maybe she just didn't know how to handle physical contact that wasn't unwanted.

In the text, it seemed as though she already knew her feelings wouldn't be reciprocated. I wasn't so sure, myself. I'd always thought that she was gorgeous, but she never quite seemed comfortable in her own skin. It was like her whole presentation was an act. Her personality though, I loved to death. Sometimes it was difficult to differentiate between the symptoms of what I'd always suspected to be PTSD and her real personality, but when we were alone I'd see it come through. The irritability and guardedness would fall away to reveal a sweet, honest human being. She was extremely passionate and kind, loyal to a fault. Despite the aggression that everyone saw as her defining trait, she was actually one of the most gentle people I'd ever met. She'd never intentionally hurt someone that wasn't already being violent. Any time she laid a hand on someone it was purely reactive. Sometimes she just took it too far.

I blinked, trying to bring myself back to my original thoughts. I kept getting sidetracked. Could I love her as more than a friend? Part of me felt like I already did. I just didn't know what to make of everything. I'd talk to her once she woke up.

The next portion of the message was significantly harder to unpack. She'd picked the right question to answer. I'd asked so many times why she chose to get involved in situations where her and I both knew she'd get herself in trouble. However, I felt like she didn't give me the whole answer. Maybe she didn't realize it herself. It made sense that she wanted to protect people from feeling the way she had. I'd always figured that she'd been hurt by someone in the past by the scars on her body and extreme reactions to being touched when she didn't want it. There was more to it than that, though. It wasn't just her not wanting other people to feel the way she had: she also valued herself less than everyone else. She didn't care about getting in trouble or a fight protecting another person, because in her mind she was worthless – the other person deserved safety more than she did. That, most of all, was the reason I hated her fighting. Every time I saw her knuckles raw and scuffed up all I could see was how little she cared about herself. How little she thought she was worth.

I read the next part three more times than all the others. In talking about not wanting others to feel the way that she had, she brought up the night when she'd pulled a guy off of me. I looked over at her, still asleep. Had someone hurt her like that? I understood why she'd refused to tell anyone. Someone had gotten the upper hand on her. She couldn't stop them. In everything she did, she so desperately wanted to be in control. Admitting that someone had taken it from her was probably the hardest thing she'd ever done. My face got hot as I remembered how I'd felt that night. I had been so scared. I'd used all my strength trying to get him off of me, but he still had me pinned and I couldn't move. Liz was so strong, she'd ripped him off of me in one motion. No one could do that to her now. She must've been young when it happened. Maybe her strength was compensation. Her refusal to tell anyone meant that she'd gone through it alone. I couldn't imagine. It had been so hard for me, and he didn't even get to do anything, and she was there for me the entire time afterwards. She'd been completely alone. Didn't tell anyone. Didn't have a family to go to. Fuck, was it the family she was with that did it? Was I the first person she'd told? She didn't even outright tell me. She'd never come right out and say something like that.

I read the whole thing one last time. It hurt my heart. She was always as real as she could be with me, but I'd never seen her be so deeply genuine. There was so much pain. She let me see more than she'd ever shown anyone else. I knew she'd struggled with a lot, but I'd never known how deep it went. She wouldn't let me. The only reason she'd sent this to me was because she thought she wasn't going to be around for the consequences. Now I had scratched the surface of how much pain she was in on a daily basis, and I wasn't going to let it go. I'd let her shut me out long enough. It was clear she couldn't do this one her own; she'd just never admit it. She was getting real help this time, whether she wanted it or not. The idea of looking weak probably scared her more than anything. I'd have to show her that getting help wasn't a weakness.

Liz shifted in the bed and groaned. I jumped, almost dropping my phone. Putting it back in my pocket, I leaned over to the side of the bed and gently picked up her hand, trying to nudge her awake. I had to keep reminding myself not to bombard her the minute she woke up. I didn't know how she was going to react once she realized what had happened. The only thing I knew for sure was that I wasn't going to take any bullshit answers, and I was going to show her that I wasn't about to give up on her.

CHAPTER SEVEN

I groaned as I started to wake up. Someone was holding my hand, but the sensation was overshadowed by a stabbing pain in my ribs and a sting in my throat. Fighting to open my eyes, I tried to look around the room and figure out where I was. There was a rhythmic beep in the background, the lights were bright, and everything smelled of antiseptic. As I lifted up my opposite hand, there was a slight tug on the back of it and I squinted as hard as I could to figure out why. It was an IV. I was in the hospital. Closing my eyes again, I tried to think back to the night before to figure out what had happened. I'd gotten into a fight, Mom brought me home from the police station. I went to the skate park...*Oh fuck.*

I was alive. I'd told Alex everything, and now I had to answer for it.

You failed. You couldn't even get this right.

There was a nudge against my arm – a soft touch from warm hands. The spark wasn't there though – what did that mean? It couldn't be anyone *but* Alex, why was the spark gone? Did she hate me so much that there wasn't any love in her touch anymore? Was she here to tell me everything was over?

"Liz?" Her voice was low and soft.

She didn't sound angry, but she sounded a lot more forced than usual. As though she was trying to hold something back. She was too nice to tell me how angry she was.

It was so hard to keep my eyes open. I wanted to slip into unconsciousness again, hide away from the world forever. Unfortunately, I knew she wouldn't let me.

How did I even get here? I'd thrown away my phone, no one could track it. I hadn't told anyone where I was going. I'd taken a large enough dose that I should've been dead in less than an hour. How did someone find me so fast? *Who* found me so fast?

Why couldn't I just fucking die and do everyone a favor?

"Liz." The same voice, but a much sharper tone. Maybe she couldn't hide her anger anymore.

I fought again to open my eyes. There was a red blur next to the bed, and vague shapes around the room. She let go of my hand, and a moment later I could see clearly. She'd slipped my glasses on my face. At least it was easier to open my eyes now.

Glancing up at her I could see dark circles and irritated eyes. She'd been crying. I made her cry. *Again.*

You're such a piece of shit.

There were scrapes on her arm that she hadn't had the day before. I would get similar ones occasionally when sneaking through broken chain-link fencing.

Was she the one that found me?

I hoped to god that she wasn't. That would just make everything so, so much worse. Who else could have though? I only texted her and Seth, and he never checked his damn messages, and wouldn't even begin to know where to find me. He knew I liked to skate but had no clue where the park was.

It was her. She'd found me. She'd called for help. And I fucking made her go through that. This was supposed to make things better for her, not worse.

You can't fucking do anything right. You still hurt people even when you're dying.

I didn't have any words for her. Just like yesterday, an apology would be insulting. There wasn't anything I could do to fix this. I could never fix this.

You ruin everything.

I squinted, trying to fight back tears. I was pathetic. Crying in front of her would just make her feel bad, I'd already done that enough. As I inhaled, a sharp pain shot through my ribcage and a squeak escaped my throat.

"Stop trying to be so fucking stoic." Her tone was sharp. The anger had made its way to the surface.

What?

"You just fucking tried to kill yourself and you're sitting here forcing yourself to not cry. Stop it! You're fucking human, stop trying to act like nothing matters to you." She'd raised her voice.

I'd never heard her yell before. I knew she'd hate me. Part of me felt like she was right though. What the fuck did it matter at this point if I cried?

You're already the biggest piece of shit there is.

I gave up trying to hold it back, and the sobs began to escape, shaking my entire body. I hated it, it felt like I had no control. Each sob sent a new pain shooting through my ribcage, making it harder to breathe and making each subsequent sob more intense. It was a never-ending cycle.

Then, she did something I'd never expected. She stood up and moved the chair away from the bed. At first, I thought she was leaving – too fed up with my shit, done with trying to be my friend. Instead, she carefully pushed my upper body up from the mattress, and slid herself behind me, wrapping her arms around my chest. She rested her chin on my shoulder and let me lean back into her. She held me tighter than I ever thought she could and let me cry until there were no more tears left.

After a long while, she spoke. "I'm not mad at you, I'm sorry I yelled. I just don't understand why you would do this." Her tone was much softer than before.

"Everyone's better off." My voice was hoarse and my throat hurt even more when I tried to talk.

Her body tensed up behind me. It felt as though her temperature rose five degrees the instant she heard those words. She took a deep breath and let it out before she spoke again.

"See, that's what I'm mad about. I'm not mad at you – I'm mad that that idea makes any kind of sense in your head. You really believe I'd be better off without you?"

I wrapped my hands around her arms. Tears were still running down my cheeks, but the sobs had subsided and it was getting easier to breathe. Her embrace was warm, comforting even. Maybe the sparks were gone because I wasn't anxious about her finding out I was in love with her? She knew almost everything now.

"You...you wouldn't be stuck here. You wouldn't be crying over me."

"Liz, that only works if I'd never met you. That ship sailed four years ago. I wouldn't even be better off then, my life at home would be just as shitty. I'd just have nowhere to go." She paused for a minute, trying to find the right way to compose her thoughts. She lowered her voice, almost to a whisper. "If you'd died last night, I...I'd be fucking devastated. I love you to death, I can't imagine my life without you.”

I didn’t know how to feel about what she was saying. I didn’t know how to feel about anything anymore. I wanted to ask about what I’d told her, but I was so afraid. Maybe she was just avoiding it so that we could pretend it didn’t happen? That wasn’t how she usually dealt with things. She wasn’t one to sweep things under the rug.

After a few more minutes of silence and me sniffling, she whispered again. “We need to talk about what you said.”

Yeah, I knew she wouldn’t leave it alone.

“I’ll be honest, I really don’t know how I feel about it. I spent so much time chasing meaningless shit that I’m not sure what it would feel like to be in something real. On top of that, there’s so much shit going on with you that I don’t think you really know who you are, what you need.”

How was I supposed to know who I was? Did people just *know* that sort of thing?

“But I do know that I love you. I love the person you are when you’re relaxed and forget about all this shit that’s going on in your head. When it’s just you and me and you get mad about how much better I am at platformer games than you, and when you laugh at me for doing shit like licking all the syrup off my plate at breakfast. I want more of that, all the time. But that doesn’t mean I don’t love you now. I’ll still love you when you’re hurting – when you can’t see past all the darkness in your mind. I’ll love every part of you.”

She held me tighter and exhaled slowly, gently pulling my hair back from my face.

“I guess...what I mean...is that I’d love to take a shot at being your girlfriend. But I need something from you first.”

Anything.

"W...what?" My breath caught in my throat, I couldn't believe this was happening.

"You *have* to let someone help you. If I let myself fall in love with you more than I already am, I really, *really* can't do this again. If I'm constantly afraid that I'll turn my back and you won't be there anymore, I'll lose my fucking mind."

God damn it, she was right. She's always been right. Mom had been right. Everyone was fucking right. I still hated the idea of going to a therapist, but I didn't think I could do this again either. I couldn't even see a future for myself beyond the hospital bed I was in right there. I'd never been able to see myself as an adult, because I'd always felt like I would die before I got there.

Tears started streaming down my face again. "O-okay... okay." It was me whispering this time.

It hurt to admit, but felt good in some weird way. To let go. I was done fighting with myself and everyone else. I didn't have the energy for it anymore.

"Okay." She said, running her hand along my shoulder. "Now get some sleep, I'll be here when you wake up."

I was exhausted – I never realized how draining it was to cry. I hadn't done it in years, so I guess I'd forgotten. In a way it was better than the pressure I felt from holding it back. At the same time I was still frustrated with myself for not being more composed, for letting someone see me so vulnerable.

You're a fucking baby.

Shut up, shut up! Why won't you leave me alone?

I shook my head, trying to get the thoughts to stop. Alex ran her hand through my hair again, leaning back into a more comfortable position for both of us. She'd probably sleep too, with how tired she looked. I reached up and held her hand tightly until my eyes began to close and I fell asleep in her arms.

———

When I woke up again, Alex was quietly talking to Mom, who was now sitting in the chair by the bed. Alex was still behind me with her arms around me, almost as if she was afraid to let go. My ribs still felt like they were on fire, but my throat felt a little better. Why did my ribs even hurt so bad? I hadn't done anything to them – I didn't even get hit when I was fighting. They hadn't hurt at all the day before.

I winced as I took a deep breath, then squinted at Mom.

Realizing I was awake, she leaned in. "Yeah, careful sweetie, you've got a couple broken ribs."

"How?" Did I get hit by a car or something? It sure felt like it.

"CPR breaks ribs, Liz. They were working on you for like half an hour," Alex answered.

Damn, I actually almost did it.

The reality started to set in, but I still didn't know how to feel about it. Part of me still thought everyone would be so much better off if I'd died. In fact, most of me did. It felt like Alex had just said those things earlier out of pity or unfounded guilt. Now I was even worse for trapping her into a relationship she didn't want because she was afraid I'd kill myself otherwise. God, I didn't want her to feel like that. How would I tell her that though? She'd deny it – wouldn't ever admit that she'd agreed to be with me out of guilt.

I really should've just died.

Thoughts started swirling around my head and tears were brimming in my eyes. Everything was so loud, I felt so awful and I wanted it to stop. A hand softly wiped away tears that had forced their way down my cheek.

"Hey," Alex cooed softly.

I didn't know what to say, so I remained silent as she tried to console me. There was no way out of the darkness I felt, everything seemed so hopeless.

Mom wrapped her hand around mine. I thought she'd be angry so I was surprised by the gesture. I still felt like I was nothing but a disappointment. She took a deep breath in and looked me in the eyes before talking.

"Honey, you need more help than we can give you at home. I think you know that. I'm going to have you admitted to psych."

That was it. The last stop foster kids took other than jail. I'd finally gotten her to want to get rid of me. That must've been the reason she wasn't angry – she was relieved she wouldn't have to deal with me anymore. I'd never see Alex again. I'd be locked up and shot up with meds every time I wasn't a placid zombie.

The tears came harder and Alex pulled me closer into her. It hurt and felt good at the same time, I never wanted her to let go. Mom squeezed my hand and rubbed my shoulder.

"Will you talk to me? I want to know what you're thinking."

Talking wouldn't help anything. She'd already decided to get rid of me. She was right though, I belonged there. I was dangerous to everyone and everything and I'd done nothing but prove that my whole life. I wished I knew how to be good. At least in psych I couldn't disappoint anyone anymore.

"I'll come see you every day." Alex's sweet voice attempted to soothe me.

"You shouldn't. You should just leave me there."

Mom pulled away at my words, seemingly surprised by the idea.

But it was Alex that spoke first, her tone much less soft than it had been before. "Fuck that. This isn't us giving up on you, you understand? This is us getting you the help you need. You'll come home after and everything will get better. I know you can't see it right now, but I'll hope for the both of us."

I was so overwhelmed. The tears came even faster.

"I love you." Her tone soft again.

CHAPTER EIGHT

I was shuffled from the hospital bed to a wheelchair once the ICU determined I was healthy enough for the transfer to psych. A security guard wheeled me through winding hallways and elevators until we finally came upon a locked door. He scanned his badge, the latch on the door released, and he ushered me inside.

I was met with several staring faces through a window in what looked to be a common room. There was a television and a few tables, but the room was otherwise bare. I hated the attention but couldn't blame them for staring, it didn't seem like there was much else to do.

They had me get up from the wheelchair and sit in an uncomfortable plastic seat next to a nurse's station where one of them came out and began recording my vital signs. Blood pressure: normal. Temperature: normal. Pulse: a little fast. I knew that from the heartbeat in my ears and my leg bouncing aggressively up and down. I was shaking, and the nurse knelt down in front of me and said something I didn't really process. I nodded, not wanting to cause trouble the minute I had arrived. She left and then returned with a cup with a small white pill inside and said something else that ended with "...will help calm you down." I took it. I didn't care what it was, I just wanted to breathe without it feeling like I was sucking air in through a straw.

The nurse stood by me and a few minutes later another woman came out and the security guard made his exit. This woman wasn't a nurse – she was dressed in typical professional clothes rather than scrubs. I didn't make eye contact; instead I stared at the floor. I still couldn't understand what anyone was saying over the pounding in my ears. I'd catch echoey bits and pieces of words but nothing that made sense. This was worse than the fog that had been consuming me on and off for most of my life. At least I could fight through that and it wasn't always so severe. There was no fighting through this. I was exhausted, but also felt like there were jolts of electricity running through me. My body wanted to go, go, go, and my brain wanted everything to come to a screeching halt.

The woman whose name I had missed gestured for me to get up and I followed her automatically, as if under a spell. She walked into the common room where the other patients averted their eyes quickly to make it seem as though they hadn't been staring. She gestured towards the television and then the rows of small tables with more uncomfortable plastic chairs. I followed her as she showed me a small kitchen with a microwave and refrigerator. She opened the cupboards and drawers to show me the contents while we were there.

A small box of tea caught my eye. It was the same kind that Mom would make when I had nightmares. I instinctively reached out right before the woman was about to close the cabinet. She stopped and smiled at me before taking a tea bag and getting a paper cup of water to microwave. We stood in silence until the microwave beeped and she handed me the cup of tea. I took it with both hands, breathing in the scent of chamomile. Things were starting to slow down.

Another gesture to follow and the woman led me down a long hallway to a room that was bare except for two beds and two small tables. The woman's voice came through clearly for the first time.

"You'll have a roommate – her name is Samantha. She's a sweet girl, I'm sure she'll show you around more once you're settled."

With that, she walked out of the room, closing the door behind her. I sat there with the cup of tea in my hands for what felt like an eternity as my heart rate slowly dropped and things began moving slower. Eventually, I stopped shaking and took a sip of the tea. It was bitter – the lady hadn't put anything in it. I liked it that way. The hot liquid poured down my throat and it fell into my stomach. It was a soothing feeling that I'd always loved about a steaming hot cup of tea.

My eyelids became heavy and the room started to spin slowly, like it was warping an inch or so every minute that I stared at it. I put the tea down on the table next to the bed where I sat and my limbs took on the same heaviness. I lay down on the bed, not even bothering to cover myself with the blanket. Within minutes, I was asleep.

———————

I awoke to a room dimly lit from the window of the door. There was a shadow in the patch of light that was cast on the floor and I jumped up with a start to see a girl sitting in the middle of the floor with a book.

"I'm sorry!" The girl's voice was low and soft.

I calmed a little bit, remembering where I was and what had happened earlier in the day. How long had I been asleep?

"I didn't know if the light would wake you and I wanted to read – I didn't think about how creepy it would look sitting in the middle of the floor in the dark." She had a slight laugh in her voice. "Is it alright if I turn the light on now?"

I nodded wearily, squinting my eyes as the jarring fluorescent light flickered on. I'd fallen asleep with my glasses on so I could immediately see the girl. She was tall, thin but muscular, had very dark skin, and had green eyes slightly darker than Alex's. She looked to be about my age. Her hair was natural in a beautiful curly afro that barely met her shoulders. She was wearing an oversized t-shirt and shorts that showed off galaxy-print leggings underneath. She wore a compassionate smile on her face. A look of understanding even though she had no idea who I was.

"What time is it?" I muttered, sleep still hinted in my voice.

The girl opened the door and poked her head out, then closed it a second later. "Ten thirty. They have us go in our rooms at ten. If you're hungry or something we can still go get food though, as long as we come right back."

I was hungry. I had come to the unit before breakfast and all I'd had was the tea. How long had I been sitting here before I got tired? Had I slept the entire day? What did that nurse give me?

My look of bewilderment must've been pretty obvious, as the girl chuckled at me. "They gave you some meds, didn't they?"

I nodded.

"Yeah, the first dose isn't usually right – it won't always be like that. They'll figure it out for you, you've just gotta tell them what happens."

My stomach growled before I could ask a question.

"You slept all day, you must be hungry. Come with me, we'll get you something."

I got up and followed the girl without question, wringing my hands as we walked down the brightly lit hallway. She brought me into the kitchen and opened all the cupboards and drawers in a similar fashion as the woman had earlier. This time I could at least focus enough to see what was happening. I decided on a peanut butter and jelly sandwich and went to work on making it.

"I'm Samantha, by the way. You can call me Sam," the girl said from a few feet away as she took out some chocolate milk. "Want some?"

I looked over and nodded, causing her to reach back in the fridge and grab another carton.

"Liz," I muttered as I put the bread away and bit into my freshly made sandwich. Sam smiled at me and then started walking back towards our room with both cartons of milk in her hands.

Sam seemed so unremarkable and friendly that I had a hard time understanding why she was here – wasn't everyone in a psych ward supposed to be completely delusional? This place didn't seem anywhere near as bad as what I'd seen in movies. My expectations had been complete chaos compared to this. Maybe I'd slept through all the commotion. Regardless, I followed Sam back to our room while stuffing my face with the sandwich in a less than graceful manner. There were guards pacing the halls – big burly-looking men that made me nervous with their presence – I'd much rather be in the room with Sam.

We sat down on our beds and Sam picked her book back up while I ate. Despite sleeping all day I was still tired. I didn't feel as heavy as I had when I'd first fallen asleep, I suspected that had been due to whatever medication the nurse had given me. I didn't want to take more of whatever it was – I was foggy enough already and that added heaviness would make functioning impossible.

Although, at this point, I don't know if you could call what I'd been doing these last few years functioning.

I lay back down, and this time I pulled the covers over myself and took my glasses off. I stared at the wall for a while as my thoughts started to swarm around me. My head had been quiet when I'd first woken up, it was nice. This was the inner chaos I was used to, but it felt so much louder now that I'd had a reprieve, however short.

I want Alex. I want to go home.

You failed, and now look where you are. No one wants you.

Tears started rolling down my cheeks. Normally I'd fight it, but I didn't care anymore. I'd given up. My skin crawled and I wanted to hurt myself. Anything to take this sensation away.

"Hey, are you alright?" Sam's voice had a coo similar to Alex's.

I didn't say anything. I didn't have the energy and I didn't want to talk, I just wanted to go back to that blackout sleep I'd had earlier. Maybe I would take that medication again. Being asleep forever was the next best thing to death.

"It's okay if you don't want to talk, Liz. But we could do something other than stare at the wall, y'know? I've got cards, we could play a game if you like."

She was sweet, but I rolled over, blowing her off. I didn't mean any offense to her, but it was just as well. She shouldn't try to help or like me, it never ended well for anyone involved. I closed my eyes, hoping I'd fall asleep again.

Sleep never came. Sam eventually turned the light off and went to bed, and after hours of laying awake absolutely hating myself for getting to this point, a nurse came in the room with the equipment to take our vitals. She started with Sam, who woke after the nurse called her name a couple times. She also handed Sam a small cup like the one I'd been given the day before, and she took it without hesitation. Then the nurse came over and had me sit up to take my vitals, but didn't offer a cup afterwards. I'd secretly been hoping that she would. Instead, she left.

I pulled my knees up to my chest. I was exhausted, but I knew if I lay back down I still wouldn't be able to sleep. Desperately, I hoped Sam wouldn't be angry with me for blowing her off the night before – I needed some distraction. Everything in my mind weighed on me so heavily and all I wanted was for it to go away.

"I'm...I'm sorry."

She gave me a quizzical look. "For what?"

I stared at the floor. Talking took so much effort. I was so tired and the fog washed over me as I tried to form a sentence. Thankfully, I didn't have to.

"You've got nothing to be sorry for. I know it's hard. I don't know exactly what you've got going on, but if it's anything like me it's a lot to work through."

I sighed. I didn't want to "work through" anything. I just wanted it to go away. The pain was so exhausting.

"Why don't you come have breakfast with me? They should be putting it out soon."

I nodded, following her as she got up and opened the door. We walked down the hallway together and went into the large common room where the other patients had been the day before. There were a couple people sitting at tables and someone was bringing in trays and setting them in front of the patients. Sam and I sat down at the table in the corner. We both sat facing the room with our backs to the wall. Soon, the person with the trays came to us and set a meal in front of each of us.

"Hi, Christy," Sam said with a chipper tone in her voice.

The woman smiled and nodded. "Good morning, Sam." She then looked at me. "Good to see you up this morning."

I nodded and picked up the plastic fork on the tray and began picking at the eggs on the plate. They weren't as bad as school food, at least.

"The doctors will meet with you today since they couldn't yesterday. They'll probably start you on some meds, but don't worry, it shouldn't be like what you got when you first got here. They'll adjust things if they're not right," Christy informed me.

More talking. I probably should've expected it, but god damn this was so hard already. I was glad things were being explained at least. I didn't like being blindsided by queries from person after person.

As if on cue, a tall, willowy man in semi-formal attire walked in the room and headed straight for our table. He smiled at me and Sam as he placed his hands on the edge.

"You must be Elizabeth." His tone was calm and slow, as if he were trying not to startle a skittish animal.

I stared up at him, offering no response.

"I'm Dr. Samuel. Would you be willing to come and meet with us for a little? You can bring your food if you like."

I looked warily at Sam. She nodded, trying to encourage me to go with the man. Placing my fork back on the tray, I picked up the cup of tea that had been set there as I got up to follow him. He walked swiftly, it was difficult to keep up and not spill my tea on the way to the door of the small office he entered. Once we got inside, there were two other doctors sitting around the table. One with his face buried in a laptop, and another who offered me a polite smile, the corners of her eyes creasing behind her thick-rimmed glasses.

Dr. Samuel closed the door and sat down across from the woman with glasses, offering me the seat at the end of the table. I sat down and carefully began tracing the rim of the paper cup with my finger. The doctor at the laptop stopped typing and looked up at me expectantly.

"Elizabeth, why don't you tell us a bit about yourself?"

Crickets rang through my head. What was I supposed to tell this man? That I was a fuck-up with no hope? How many times I hurt others? How many times I hurt myself? The list was too long, there were too many mistakes. I wished they'd just drug me and be on their way.

After a long silence, the man behind the computer cleared his throat. "How about we start with what brought you in here?"

My body tensed up and my leg started bouncing involuntarily. I continued tracing the rim of the cup and didn't look up.

"I tried to kill myself." My voice flat, monotone.

"And what were you feeling when you made that decision?"

I shrugged.

Dr. Samuel leaned towards me and with the same too-cautious tone in his voice said, "Elizabeth, no one's going to judge you here. We're here to help, but we can't help if you don't talk to us. I know it's hard, but you've got to trust us a little."

"I don't know...sad? Worthless?"

"What made you feel sad and worthless?"

"Everything."

"Would you say that you have those feelings often?"

"I guess...and angry."

"What happens when you get angry?"

"I hurt people. Or myself."

"Do you ever use drugs to get away from these feelings?"

"Yes."

"What drugs?"

"Alcohol, weed...and sometimes heavy stuff."

My chest was getting tight and I was starting to shake. The man typing on the computer was so loud that I could hear it echo through my brain. The questions stopped for a minute as the doctors exchanged looks. I wanted to get up and run out of the room, never look back. Eventually, the questions began again. A relentless grilling for information.

"What are you feeling right now?"

"I want it to stop."

"Want what to stop?"

"Everything."

The doctor with the glasses leaned towards me and I jerked back. What were they writing about me? Was I too fucked up even for them? Were they going to keep me in here forever? Tears started to force their way out of the corners of my eyes.

The doctor behind the computer went on as if nothing happened. "Do you ever experience anxiety?"

I nodded.

"Are you feeling anxious now?"

I nodded again.

"Do you have a history of trauma?"

No. I'm done.

I got up and ran out of the room, leaving my cup of tea behind. I ran into the bedroom, closing the door behind me and curled into a ball in bed and cried. I couldn't do this. Everything was too much. I pulled in jagged breaths as the sobs forced their way out of me. I'd never cried like this before, it was uncontrollable.

It was so hard to breathe and everything around me was spinning. I started coughing as my breath escaped me. I was being so loud, everyone would know how pathetic I was.

Why couldn't you have done the job right in the first place? You're too much to deal with.

I want to die. I wanna die. Let me die.

"Elizabeth?" Dr. Samuel's voice was barely audible over the screaming in my head.

He knelt down beside the bed – I had my back turned to him but I was sure he knew I was crying. I tried desperately to stop but couldn't. In fact, it seemed as though the tears came harder the more I resisted. Curling tighter into myself, I tried to disappear from the world.

Dr. Samuel shifted but didn't leave. He waited me out silently, letting me have my feelings. After about ten minutes I finally got the sobs under control a little and rolled over to see him sitting on the floor with a concerned look on his face.

"Good job calming down a little. Can you take a few deep breaths with me?"

I nodded, sitting up and pulling my knees tight to my chest.

"Okay, we'll breathe in, one...two...three...four. And hold it, one...two...three...four...five...six. And out, one...two...three...four... five...six...seven...eight. Good. And again."

We breathed like that for a few minutes until the last of my sobs subsided and I was able to take in the breath without struggling. He gave me a smile.

"Good job. I understand that all the questions were a little too much for you, and it's okay. We just need to get some kind of general information so we can start figuring out what kind of medication you might benefit from. Clearly you carry a lot of anxiety – but that last question was pretty important. Can you just give me a yes or no and we'll be done for today?"

I nodded yes.

"Okay. Thank you for trying so hard. We'll give you something for the anxiety, and discuss what might work best for your other symptoms. Based on your history and what you've told us, I suspect you may have Post-Traumatic Stress Disorder."

I stared at him. No one had ever diagnosed me before, so I don't know what I'd been expecting, but it wasn't that. I'd always been labeled as "aggressive" or "defiant." Never "traumatized" or "stressed."

"Whenever you get overwhelmed like that, I want you to try those breaths we did, okay? It should help. For now, why don't you go back in the common room with Samantha and do something to keep your mind busy?"

"Okay," I managed to squeak out.

Dr. Samuel stood up and I followed him as he walked out of the room. He took a turn into the small room where we had been meeting and waved for me to continue on to the common room. I walked in and sat down next to Sam and stared at the half-eaten tray of food that was now missing the tea I really wanted.

"How'd you do?" Sam asked, leaning forward to get a good look at my face through my thick bangs.

"Shitty," I muttered.

She sighed. "It's okay. The first time's always really tough, it's a lot of questions."

She looked at me for a minute and must've seen the tear streaks and redness in my face.

"How about that card game?"

"Okay," I said, pushing the tray of food away from me.

Sam smiled and pulled a deck of cards from a nearby shelf and started shuffling. Sitting across from me and moving the tray out of the way, she dealt out a hand for rummy. I picked up the cards and fanned them out in my hand. We started playing and she chuckled when I quickly beat her in the first round.

"You're pretty good at this, I play a lot of rummy."

"Had a foster dad who taught me a lot of card games."

She smiled, "Was he a good one?"

"Yeah. He taught me to skateboard, too. I had to leave because one of their bio kids got in an accident and the social workers said they wouldn't have enough time for me anymore. I was too much work."

"That's shitty, I'm sorry."

I shrugged.

"Do you know if you'll have any visitors? Hours start soon."

"I dunno."

Inside I was hoping against everything that Alex would come like she said, even though my mind was still telling me that no one should waste their time on me like that.

We played a few more hands until the locked door leading outside the unit opened and some people I didn't recognize came in. The nurses showed them into the common room where they met with patients. I didn't see Alex. Disappointment ran through me and I slouched farther down in the uncomfortable seat. The door opened again and I almost didn't look up, but something possessed me to. I saw a flash of fire red hair. Dropping the cards, I got up and ran towards the door, throwing my arms around Alex and burying my face in her chest.

"Hey," she said softly, "I tried to see you yesterday, but they said you were sleeping. Are you okay?"

I never wanted her to leave again. She smelled so good, like vanilla and pomegranates. She was so warm and it felt good as she embraced me, despite the residual soreness in my ribs. She rubbed my back until one of the nurses came up and loudly cleared her throat.

"That's enough," she said in a sharp tone.

I still didn't want to let go, but the nurse made me nervous. Afraid she'd make Alex leave, I pulled away and instead interlaced my fingers in hers. We walked into the common room and sat down at a table when I noticed – no one had come for Sam. She was sitting alone, playing a game of solitaire like she hadn't expected anyone in the first place. A part of me wondered how long she'd been here.

Alex caught my attention by running a hand though my hair and I lost my focus on Sam.

"You didn't answer me, how're you doing?"

I looked down at the light-green blouse she was wearing and wrapped my hands around her waist before speaking. "It's really hard. I miss you."

"I know, honey. It's gonna be hard for a little bit, but it'll get better. I promise. Okay?"

I nodded, not really believing her but also hanging on every word she said.

"Did they start giving you meds yet?"

"They gave me something yesterday, that's why I slept all day. I think they're gonna give me different stuff now, but they haven't yet. One of the doctors said I had PTSD."

She stroked my hair. "I hope they find something that helps, you don't deserve to be feeling so shitty and I know you've felt that way for a long time. I think they're probably right, honey.

You've been through so much that you don't talk about."

I laid my head down on her shoulder and she kissed the top of it. I wanted so desperately to go home with her and stay there forever. She rubbed circles in my back with one hand and brushed the hair out of my face with the other. It was so much easier to breathe with her there. I'd never understand how she could manage to make me feel so safe no matter where we were.

"I love you," I said, tracing the pattern on her leggings with my fingers. "I'm sorry I hurt you."

"Hurt me how?"

"When I tried to...you know. I shouldn't have told you like that. I'm sorry I was too scared to tell you everything."

She let out a small sigh. "You don't need to be sorry to me. You've got to understand that you're worth more than that. I wish there was an easy way for you to believe that you're worthy of love. I know you're in so much pain, I just want to help you get through it." She held me tighter.

"I love you so much that it hurts, I don't know how to deal with it." My voice wavered.

"Well, now you don't have to do it alone."

We sat there for a while with her rubbing circles in my back as the annoyed nurse from earlier hovered around us. I didn't care, this was all I ever wanted and it felt so good to finally have it.

"Visiting hours are over," the nurse announced a few minutes later.

"Noo..." I realized in that moment that I sounded like a whiny child arguing with their mother. Alex giggled at that.

"I'll come see you tomorrow, I promise."

She leaned in and gave me a kiss that I savored until she pulled away. I slowly let her hand go as she got up and left. We waved as she was led out the locked door by a security guard.

I sat there in silence for a moment, just taking everything in. This was real. She really wanted to be with me. I had a hard time believing it and still felt a pang of guilt as though she had some obligation to be doing this. Feeling my thoughts going down a dark path, I shook my head and looked over to where Sam was sitting. I went over and sat down across from her.

"Your girlfriend's really pretty," she said with a teasing smile.

The gears in my mind spun with no traction. "I'm not... She's not...I mean, I guess she...yeah."

Sam laughed at my stuttering. "You came out recently, huh?"

"Very." I muttered.

She smiled and without looking up from her card game revealed, "I'm trans."

I squinted at her, "Really?"

She nodded. "Ask me anything, I'm always here for the baby queers."

"How did you...how did you know you were a girl?"

"How do you know you're a girl?" She quipped back.

"I don't..." I stared down at the table, scraping my fingernails against the plastic.

"Ohh, so you think you might not be?" Her tone shifted.

I shrugged.

"Well, I kind of always felt like a girl. I liked what people typically think of as girly things, I wanted to be around other girls, I've always been pretty feminine. You don't have to be super feminine to be a girl though. Have you ever had dysphoria?"

"What's that?"

"Certain parts make you feel super uncomfortable, there's a disconnect between your mind and body. For me it's a really icky sensation in whatever part I feel is wrong, crawling almost, like a growth that shouldn't be there. Or socially, if someone calls me 'he' it feels like a punch in the gut."

"I don't like my chest...or my hair...or my curves...I hate my name...but I don't think I feel like a boy either? I don't feel like anything."

"There's more than just boy or girl, you know?"

I looked up from the spot on the table I had been picking at, "Really?"

"Yeah! If you don't really feel like anything, you might be agender, which is neither. There's demiboys, who are kinda in between but more on the boyish side, there's a whole bunch."

My mind reeled. I'd never heard of any of this. Agender? Having feminine traits attached to me had always felt so wrong, and the idea of masculine traits didn't sit much better.

"You said agender is neither?"

"Yep. You don't have to present any specific way, but a lot of people prefer to look more androgynous. It sounds like looking feminine makes you pretty uncomfortable. Have you ever experimented with your presentation at all?"

"No...I always kinda wear oversized stuff and my hair's been the same since I was a little kid."

She smiled. "Maybe when you get out of here you can play around with that a little? You could get a binder and cut your hair if you wanted."

"A binder?"

"It's kind of like this tank top that compresses and gives you a flatter chest."

My eyes widened. I'd never heard of it, but that sounded *amazing*. I'd always been heavy-chested and I absolutely hated it.

Every hoodie I owned was two sizes too big to hide it.

"Maybe your girl can help give you a makeover."

I chuckled a little. She'd probably like that.

"In the meantime, you said you hated your name. Why not pick a new one?"

CHAPTER NINE

"River?"

"Nah."

"Finley?"

"No."

"Tatum?"

"Ew."

We read down a list of gender-neutral names Sam had asked one of the doctors to print out.

"Kirby." Sam laughed.

"Come on." I rolled my eyes.

"Theo."

"Theo," I repeated, testing the name in my mouth.

She smiled. "You like that one?"

I grinned for the first time in what felt like months. "Yeah. I like it a lot."

"You're Theo then."

I had to admit, I was *excited.* This felt right. Nothing about me had ever felt right, and now it was as if a weight had been lifted off of me. I was anxious at the same time – would my friends and family be okay with this? Would Alex be okay with it? I'd just admitted to liking girls, would this be too much?

"Uh oh, you're having the queer crisis, aren't you?" Sam interrupted my spiraling thoughts.

"What?"

"You've got a face. You're freaking out over how people will react, aren't you?"

"A little."

She chuckled, "That's normal. My best advice there is that the good ones will stick around. Your girl seemed like a good one from what I could see. Let yourself be happy with who you are for a minute before freaking out over what other people think."

"What if everyone leaves? What if my mom doesn't want me anymore? I'm already a lot to deal with."

"My parents are lawyers and if they can deal with having a trans dancer for a daughter, I think your mom will be alright. I can't tell you for sure that everything will work out perfectly, but a lot of times reality is a lot less harsh than what's in your head."

"Elizabeth?" A nurse called from down the hall.

God, now that I'd realized why I hated my name so much it really did feel like a punch in the gut. I turned to look and a heavy-set, sweet-looking nurse was walking towards me with two paper cups in her hands. She had rosy cheeks and deep brown eyes.

"Here, the doctors just put in the order for these."

She handed me a cup with two pills that varied in shape and color. This time, I decided not to take them without questioning anything first.

"What are they?"

"The round white one is Lexapro, which should help with your general symptoms. The orange capsule is neurontin, which should help with your anxiety. The doctors might change or add things as they get to know you better, but this is what they've decided to start with."

"Will they make me sleep all day like the other thing did?"

"No, hon. I believe they gave you Haldol the other day, which is for extreme symptoms and tends to make people pretty sleepy. These might make you a little tired, but it shouldn't be anywhere near as sedative."

I nodded at her and took the pills. She gave me a smile and then walked away, and I turned back to Sam.

She nodded towards the nurse, "I've been on both of those before – they didn't work for me. But they shouldn't make you too tired, you get used to it."

I sat down in one of the stiff plastic chairs. Sam was sitting in an uncomfortably impossible position with her limbs sprawled over the arms.

"How long have you been here?" I asked, making eye contact for once.

"A month, but it's not my first time."

"Did your parents send you here because…"

"I'm trans?" She chuckled. "No, my parents are actually really supportive. I'm bipolar – I have some pretty mixed episodes, but this time I was really manic – thought I could tame wild animals." She shook her head with an exasperated look. "Would've been pretty cool if true."

"So you didn't try to kill yourself?" I thought there was only one way people got here.

"Nah, not this time," She cocked her head at me. "Did you?"

I didn't answer. Staring down at the table, I found a piece of glue to pick at.

"Do you love her?"

"What?"

"Do you love your girl? I know there's that whole 'love yourself before others can love you' thing but I've always thought it was bullshit gatekeeping that neurotypicals put on love. Sometimes it can give you something to hold on to when things are hard."

"I...I did a shitty thing."

Sam looked at me expectantly.

"I texted her right before I did it...that was when I told her how I felt."

"Hold up." She shifted in the chair and leaned in towards me, lowering her voice. "You mean to tell me that your suicide note was a love letter? You're right, that...that's a little fucked."

I picked at the glue some more. "When I woke up, she told me that she loved me too and now I just feel like shit, like she thinks she has to be with me or I'll do something again."

"That's...yeah. That's tough. Have you talked to her about it?"

"Not really. I apologized and she said it was okay but that was it."

"You should have like, a good conversation with her about it. That's important."

"I'm afraid she'll lie to make me feel better."

"Does she make a habit out of lying to you? Because that's a whole 'nother problem."

"No, she's a really bad liar."

"Well, there you go. If she lies, you let her go, because that's not healthy for either of you."

"I'm scared, I don't want to lose her."

"Let me tell you, any girl that visits her other in the psych ward isn't in it just for the niceties. It's a conversation you need to have, but the way she acts with you, I don't think it'll have a bad outcome. She's into you."

I sighed, picking the last of the glue off the table. She was right, I just didn't want to do it. At least I could put it off until tomorrow, I wouldn't see Alex again until then. I was exhausted from not sleeping and everything that happened today. Hopefully I'd sleep that night.

Talking like this was so out of my realm, but here it felt like it didn't matter. Everyone had done something to get themselves in here, and we'd never see each other again after this. Talking to Sam was relieving in a way – she was real. She didn't bullshit anything for your feelings but she was kind about it at the same time. She was the kind of friend you'd go to if you wanted real answers instead of a simple ego boost.

"Theo."

I looked up and felt blood rush into my cheeks. A grin forced its way across my lips. It was the first time someone had ever called me by my new name.

Sam clapped her hands together and smiled at me. "That's how you know it's your name."

My laughter was cut short by the shout of a man in the hallway. He'd just been brought in through the security door and was fighting against the guards. He was visibly drunk, his face beet red and movements sloppy. My anxiety kicked up as the guards tried to get him under control. A heap of large men in a physical altercation. His drunken shouts rang through my head and my breathing started to spiral.

"Hey, Theo, it's okay. They'll—"

I was already gone. Taken off running down the hallway, no destination in mind. Just *away*.

"Hey!" someone shouted at me.

I ignored it, running to the end of the hallway where I was cornered by another large man in scrubs.

No no no.

"Fuck you! Fuck you all!" The drunken man shouted from the other end of the hallway.

I covered my ears, and the man in scrubs took a step closer.

"Don't touch me," I warned and begged at the same time.

The man got closer still and then I wasn't in control of my movements, it was pure survival instincts. I punched him in the gut, *hard*. Hands grabbed me and I started flailing, desperate to get out, away, anywhere but here. Somewhere safe. I fought with all my strength against them and more hands came down on me, pinning me to the ground.

Bang.

I hit the back of my head on the floor, hard. If I wasn't conscious I wouldn't feel them hurt me. I slammed my head into the floor a few more times and shouts surrounded me. They struggled to flip me over onto my stomach. Four, maybe five pairs of hands.

Bang.

They can't hurt me if I'm not awake.

My forehead hit the cold tile. I was screaming. At least, I think it was me. I couldn't feel it. The room was spinning, my ears ringing. I fought, and fought, and fought.

A sharp pinch in my leg. Everything spinning, hands easing off of me as my body relaxed against my will. Things growing fuzzy, my sight getting darker.

I traced my hands along the wood grain in my hiding spot. The world crashed and shook around me. A plate hit the door of the cupboard I was inside and shattered, creating a large thud that made me yelp, revealing my location to the aggressor. The door flew open and a calloused, sweaty hand grabbed my arm. I was so light that I was yanked out instantaneously.

"The fuck are you doin'?" the large, balding man shouted in my face.

I wanted to run, but the man had a vice-like grip on my arm that was sure to leave a bruise. My inability to run prompted tears to start flowing down my cheeks as the man's rancid breath blew across my face. All I could smell was whiskey and rot. He dug his grimy fingernails into my skin.

"Fuckin' bitch." The man released his grip and pushed me away, causing me to fall to the ground.

I scrambled to my feet, got away as quickly as I could, and hid behind the door frame. The man continued tearing through the kitchen, looking for something. Suddenly, he froze on an open bag of potato chips. He wheeled around and charged straight at me. I tried to flee but he was bigger, stronger, faster. He grabbed me again and I screamed.

"Did you fuckin' do this?" He yelled, waving the bag of chips that he'd opened in a drunken stupor the night before.

I shook my head vigorously as he grasped me tighter. It felt like he might break my arm.

"You lyin' bitch! You're always gettin' into my food!"

He slapped me across the face and I yelped. My cheek stung where he'd hit me, but I was quickly distracted from that as he grabbed me by the neck. I struggled against him and screamed until he'd constricted my throat so much that nothing came out. I flailed wildly and grabbed at his arms in a futile attempt to release his grip from me. Everything started to go black.

"Elizabeth!"

I awoke with a scream still on my lips to several people standing around my bed including a nurse, a security guard, and Sam who looked the most concerned of all. Trying to catch my breath, I sat up and leaned forward. That's when I realized I was in restraints. My arms and legs were tied to the bed and my heart felt like it was going to beat right out of my chest. I couldn't run, I couldn't fight, I couldn't breathe.

A woman dressed in casual clothing stepped closer to the bed. "*Cálmate*, por favor."

My attention snapped onto her. Everything stopped for a split second.

"Good. I'll get you out of these restraints, you just can't go hitting anyone again, okay?"

I nodded, staring at the woman like I was in a trance. She was maybe a little bit taller than me with dark, shoulder-length hair. She had such a serene air about her, it was contagious.

She undid the restraints on my arms and I put my hands up to my throat, trying to shake the ghostly feeling of tightness that remained from my dream. Tears forced their way into my eyes and blurred my vision.

"It was a dream. You're safe here. Everything's okay." She said, pulling a chair closer to my bed and sitting down.

I tried the breaths the doctor had taught me earlier and after a few was able to breathe normally. My entire body was still shaking, but at least I wasn't struggling to take in air anymore.

"Have you had nightmares like this before?" the woman asked.

I nodded, warily eyeing the security guard who was standing a little too close for my comfort. He was a tall, burly man and I really wasn't fond of men twice my size. As if realizing my apprehension, he took a step back, giving me a little more space.

Running my hands along my arms, I felt a sting as I realized there were scratches and bruises up and down them, probably from the altercation earlier. I sighed. Why did it have to be like this?

The woman nodded to the security guard and nurse and they made their exit. She then turned back to me.

"My name's Carmen. I'll be the therapist working your case. Do you want to talk?"

"How...how did you know to use Spanish?" I squeaked out. My throat was hoarse – how long had I been screaming?

"It was in your file that you'd refused to speak English in some of your earlier homes, so I decided to test a theory." She leaned back in the chair, throwing an arm over the back.

Sam sat back down on her bed and picked up her book, trying her best to give us privacy. I felt bad that I'd woken her up like that. I pulled my knees up to my chest, hiding my face against my legs. I muttered incomprehensibly into myself and then looked up at Carmen.

"Can I get some tea?"

"Sure," she said in a too-chipper tone for the hour. She then got up and left the room.

I turned to Sam. "I'm sorry."

She shrugged. "Don't be – it sounded a lot worse for you anyway. I'm an insomniac, I wasn't even asleep yet."

"I'm sorry about before too."

"Well, hey, you didn't punch *me*. Booty juice took you right out, huh?"

"Booty juice?"

She laughed, "Yeah, the shot they gave you. They use it when people get aggressive."

"Oh." I said, noticing the floating sensation in my head. "Is that why I feel weird?"

"Probably. Don't go punching anymore guards."

Carmen returned with a cup of chamomile tea. I took it gingerly and took a sip. The warmth radiated down my throat and into my stomach. Taking a deep breath in, I sighed. I sat there with my hands wrapped around the steaming hot cup.

"Elizabeth—"

"Theo. I want to be called Theo."

Sam smirked behind her book. "You go, baby queer."

"Okay, Theo. How often do you have nightmares like this?"

"I dunno." I shrugged, "a couple times a week."

"Do they keep you from sleeping?"

"Yeah. Sometimes...sometimes I use so I can sleep without them."

"How often do you do that?"

"It used to be a few times a week, but I stopped a couple months ago until...yeah."

"What made you stop?"

"My...friend caught me. We talked and I said I would stop."

"All it took was a talk?" She raised an eyebrow at me.

"I love her," I muttered.

"So you can stop for someone else, but not yourself? Do you feel like you're worth less than others?"

"I guess."

"Tell me about what happened before the nightmare. Why did you hit the guard?"

"I...I didn't mean to. The drunk guy was yelling, and I got scared and then he cornered me. I just wanted him away from me."

"Ah. So you got triggered by another patient and then felt like you had to defend yourself?"

"Yeah...I guess."

She nodded, then glanced at her watch. "Why don't you try and get some sleep? You'll be meeting with me officially tomorrow, so we'll have plenty of time to talk."

Fun. I watched as Carmen put the chair back in the corner of the room and walked out the door, smiling at me as she went. I put my tea down and looked over at Sam. She looked up from her book.

"Wanna play cards?"

———

I sat across from Carmen as she gave me an empathetic glance. Now that I was seeing her in the daylight, she didn't look like what I expected of a therapist. She was fairly young – mid to late twenties maybe. Her deep-brown shoulder-length bob framed her elegant features. I avoided eye contact. How was I supposed to just lay out my whole life's problems to her? I didn't even know where to start and couldn't imagine speaking the darkest memories into existence. Staying in my world where nothing felt real seemed like the better option.

Alex had told me that I would have to talk for things to get better. I knew she was right, but talking was so damn *painful.* My whole body was already shaking and I hadn't said a word.

I have to. I have to do this so I can leave.

"Theo, I didn't get a chance to ask last night. Do you want to use different pronouns?"

"They."

"Okay, that's easy enough." She smiled. "What prompted the change?"

"'Girl' never felt right. I just didn't know I could be anything else."

My eyes darted around the room, unable to focus on any one thing in the cluttered office. Books lined shelves that wrapped around the office. Games were stacked in a neat pile next to a desk. Many pictures of varying artistic ability framed the walls. It was homey, lived in. Not the bleak couch and chair spectacle I'd expected.

I realized incredibly late that the woman had asked me a question in my wandering.

"Theo?"

"Sorry," I muttered.

"It's alright. Is there anything in particular you wanted to talk about today?"

"Not really…" I picked at the wicker chair I was sitting in, not eager to start this process.

"Do you like games?" She gestured towards the stack next to the desk and then looked back at me.

Anything to avoid talking. "Sure."

I picked out Monopoly, long and tedious. Hopefully long enough to eat up all the time in this office. We set up the game – I picked the dog, she picked the dinosaur. Dealing out the money, she asked. "Do you get any visitors?"

"My girlfriend." It felt more natural to say each time I said it.

She smiled. "You been together long?"

"Not really. We've been friends for years, but I just told her how I felt a couple weeks ago."

"How long have you had feelings for her?"

She thought she was slick. I should've known she'd sneak therapy in somehow. At least this felt a little more natural than the direct inquiries of the psychiatrists. I went along with it. It was worth a shot.

"Since the beginning."

"Wow, so you held onto that for years?"

"Yeah."

"Do you tend to hold onto things like that?"

"I don't like talking about the hard stuff."

"I understand. Have you ever talked about the really hard stuff with anyone before?"

"No."

"That's really tough then. How about we make a plan? We pick one thing that weighs on you each session, okay? And if you get overwhelmed at any point, we can take a break and just focus on the game. Does that sound fair?"

"I guess."

"Good," she said, handing me the stack of fake money. "Your turn."

I knew she wasn't just talking about the game, but I pretended not to be keen to her intentions and rolled the dice, moving my little metal dog forward five spaces and buying the railroad. Then I handed her the dice.

She took the dice and looked at me. She knew exactly what I was doing, and she wasn't going to let me get off easy. I sighed.

"I dunno. I guess a lot of stuff comes from my bio father."

She took it. She rolled the dice, but not before asking,

"What was your relationship with him like?"

"I only remember bad stuff."

"Bad stuff like what?"

"He would drink and then hit me and yell at me a lot...I got taken away when I was six."

My hands started shaking as she handed me back the dice. I dropped them involuntarily and scrambled to pick them back up, trying to look composed. She put her hand over one of the dice, forcing me to look up at her.

"Don't worry about looking tough in here. Nothing leaves this room, and it's literally my job not to judge you. Not that I even want to."

She handed me the die. I took a deep breath to steady myself. She watched me as I took my turn, my discomfort clearly showing.

"What's happening in your body right now?"

"'I'm hot. My heart feels like it's running a mile."

"Does that happen often when you think about your birth father?"

"I guess...I try not to think about it."

"I see. It seems like you've done your best to avoid things that make you uncomfortable. The problem with that is that it doesn't go away – it just piles up until it's too much to handle. The only way out is through, kiddo."

I passed the dice over to her and leaned back, staring at the floor. My mind raced through so many scenarios I'd done my best to block out.

It's all your fault.

He grabbed me by the front of my shirt and pulled me into the overwhelming scent of whiskey that surrounded him.

"You hear me?! It's all because of you! She got sick taking care of you!"

His spit landed on my face, mixing with the tears that were flowing down my cheeks. My body was tense and my breath escaped me. I whimpered as he held me in place.

"Get out of my fuckin' sight." He released me. "Worthless. Never should've had you."

"Theo?"

I snapped back to the floor where I was sitting, tears rolling down my cheeks.

"Where did you go just now?"

"I...I'm..." I stuttered, having a hard time breathing.

This one hadn't come up in a while, and it was hitting me like a train. All at once I couldn't breathe, and sobs that I couldn't control started to overtake me. This was too much. Everything was too much.

"Try and take some deep breaths. Can you tell me what color the couch is?"

What?

The question didn't make sense to me, but I did my best to follow instructions anyway. I was trying so hard to breathe normally, but each time the air got away from me, as if my lungs were rejecting it.

Turning around to look at the couch, I gave Carmen her answer. "Gr-green."

"Good. Now what color is my shirt?"

I turned back to her and squinted, trying to focus on what was in front of me. "White."

"How many houses are on the board?"

Looking down at the board, I counted. "Two..."

"Are things slowing down?"

They were. My breathing was still labored, but the room didn't feel like it was spinning out of control anymore. Everything felt slightly more manageable. I looked up at the therapist, confused by this mind trick she'd just played on me.

She gave me a weak smile. "That's called a grounding technique. Naming things out loud helps to bring you back to the room. Makes things feel more solid. I want you to try that when you feel like you're losing reality, okay?"

I nodded. Looking back down at the game board and internally counting the number of hotels that were off to the side, I slowly regained control of my breathing.

Twelve.

She waited until I regained my composure and then asked, "Can you tell me where you just went?"

"He said it was my fault."

"Your birth father?"

"Yeah."

"Said what was your fault?"

"My mom died."

She squinted. "How old were you?"

"Four."

"Now, how could a parent's death be a four-year-old's fault?"

"I got her sick."

"That's not in your control, that's no one's doing. Do you believe it was your fault?"

I shrugged, looking back down at the game board. I saw the ruse for what it was now. These games weren't meant to actually be played, they were distractions to get you to talk. Clever.

"It's pretty common for a child to feel like their parent's

absence is their fault, no matter how it happens. The thing is, it's almost never true. I can see how being told that by your father can amplify those feelings though."

I stared into space. This wasn't getting any easier like people said it would. Maybe I was expecting too much too fast. I sure didn't feel any better. What good was bringing up things that couldn't be changed? I was tired. So, so tired. Tears came and I didn't even bother to try and stop them. Putting my hands over my face, I let the sobs overtake me. I didn't fight it.

Carmen was quiet. She waited patiently and let me cry. She didn't tell me to stop, or that there was no reason to cry. No, she knew that there was plenty reason. Exhausted, I didn't have the energy to fight anymore.

Fuck this. Fuck it all.

Carmen brought me a bottle of water, and after a long while I ran out of tears. I took the water and took a sip, placing it back down next to me. My shoulders slumped and I brought my knees up to my chest, wrapping my arms around my legs.

"I think we've done enough for today. Does that sound okay?"

I nodded, my tear-streaked face holding a neutral expression.

"You did a really good job. I know it might not feel like it, but this is progress. It's hard and it's messy and it might not feel like it right away, but it's still progress."

I got up and went back to my room, leaving Carmen's office in a silent daze. Flopping down on the bed, I curled up, clutching the pillow. Almost instantly, I fell asleep.

CHAPTER TEN

I awoke to Sam kneeling next to me, the sound of her voice pulling me from my dreamless sleep.

"Theo?"

"Ugh…"

"Alex is here. They were gonna have her leave but I said I'd get you, that you'd want to see her."

Pushing myself up off the bed, I steadied my balance as I sat up. I blinked as I willed for the room to stop spinning.

Sam squinted. "Are you okay?"

"Dizzy," I muttered.

Handing me the bottle of water beside my bed, she offered, "The meds they gave you might do that at first. Take some sips and don't get up too fast, it should pass."

I drank and then leaned back against the wall until the room gradually began to right itself. Blinking away the rest of the dizziness, I stood up slowly.

"Is it always gonna be like this?"

"It shouldn't. Your body should adjust and then it won't be so bad."

She caught me as I wavered a bit. I steadied myself against her, taking a deep breath in. She walked by my side to the common room where Alex was sitting at a table, staring out the window. She turned her head and smiled when she saw me, causing my heart to skip a beat. An involuntary grin broke out across my face as I approached her. I sat and Sam left us to our visit.

"You made a friend!" Alex said with a smile.

I rolled my eyes.

"No, that's good! I'm glad you're not all alone in here."

"Yeah…" I trailed off, not wanting to bring up what I knew I had to.

"What's wrong?"

"We...we have to talk."

She reached out and grasped my hands in hers.

I took a deep breath before starting, "I shouldn't have told you the way that I did. It was wrong."

"Told me what?"

"How I felt about you."

"Oh, Liz…"

I bristled against the name, realizing I also hadn't told her anything I'd been discussing with Sam.

"I don't want you to feel like you have to be with me. Like I'll hurt myself if you're not. I promise I won't. Not because of that."

"That's not why I'm with you." She squeezed my hands.

"Are you sure?"

"Do you really think there's no other reason I'd be with you? You sell yourself short."

I didn't say anything. The truth was, I really had no idea why else she would be with me. I knew I wouldn't want to be around myself more than I had to.

"You're really gonna make me do this?" A mischievous smile told me that she wanted to anyway. "You're one of the sweetest people I've ever met. You care about me more than anyone I've ever known, and you'd do anything to protect me. You make me feel safe in a way that no one else can. I love being around you."

My face reddened and I stared down at the table.

"It also helps that you're hot as fuck," she quipped.

"Alex!" My voice cracked and she giggled at my exasperation.

"I promise, I'm not with you out of obligation."

A weight lifted from me. I rubbed her hands with mine and sighed, "Okay."

She leaned back, barely keeping her hands within my reach.

"There's something else." My leg started bouncing as anxiety grew within me.

"What is it?"

"I'm...I..." It felt like all the air had left the room. My throat started to close and tremors overtook my body. What if she decided I was a freak? What if she left and never came back? Tears forced their way into my eyes and I pulled my hands away to cover my face.

"Hey, it's okay. Whatever it is, we can make it okay."

"I'm not a girl." Came out muffled through my hands.

Alex was silent, either in astonishment or waiting for me to keep going. I couldn't tell.

"The girl that came with me...she's been talking to me about gender stuff a lot and...I think I'm trans." The words spilled out of me like a waterfall.

"So you feel like a boy?"

"Not exactly, I think I'm neither. Is it okay if I'm neither?"

Alex leaned forward and gently pulled one of my hands

away from my face that was now a red and tear-streaked mess. She got up and pulled her chair next to me, wrapping her arms around me and kissing my forehead.

I'd been crying so much lately, I didn't know how I had any tears left. It felt like all I'd done the past week is cry. I hated Alex seeing it. I wanted to be strong for her and it felt like I was exuding nothing but weakness.

Through my broken facade, I forced out, "Will you call me Theo?"

She leaned back, keeping her arms tight around me. "Theo," she whispered, pressing her forehead to mine. "I like it. It suits you." She flashed her beautiful smile.

I reached up and put my hand against her cheek, kissing her on the lips. I couldn't help it. Her smile could melt the coldest hearts. She kissed me back, moving her hands up to my face. It was a long kiss, interrupted only by the same nurse as yesterday clearing her throat loudly behind us. Alex looked at her and rolled her eyes, while my focus was still lost in the moment of her soft kiss.

She knew now. She wasn't even the slightest bit upset, and she even liked my name. I felt like so much heaviness left me. There were still a lot of people left to come out to, but I didn't care. Alex still loved me. That was all I wanted.

"It makes a lot of sense," she said, brushing my long hair out of my face. "You've never seemed comfortable in your skin."

"I want to use they/them pronouns." I was starting to get excited now that I knew she accepted me as I was.

"Do you want to change anything?"

I grabbed a fistful of my long, coarse, dark hair. "I want to get rid of this. I want it short."

She grinned. "Oh, you'd be so fucking cute. You've got such a good face for it. I've always hated the way you hide behind your hair. You're too pretty – er – handsome for it. Is handsome okay?"

I beamed. "I like handsome." Pausing for a minute, I studied her face that mirrored my enthusiasm. "Will you help me pick out a haircut?"

"Absolutely." She pulled my hair back from my face, pushing it behind and out of view. A small giggle escaped her. "Your freckles are so cute."

I sighed and leaned into her hands, closing my eyes. God, I wanted nothing more than to go home with her. Tracing her jawline with my fingers, I stared at her features. Piercing bright green eyes that you could get lost in. Soft, curved lips that invited yet another kiss.

"Visiting time is over," the bitter nurse called out.

This time, it was me that shot her a dirty look. I followed Alex as she was led to the door, encircling her waist with my arms as she paused before leaving. I never wanted the hug to end, but all too soon she was ushered out and I was left standing against the locked door, wishing to be on the other side.

Glumly, I walked to the table where Sam was sitting and fell into the chair across from her with a complete disregard for how hard the plastic was. The jolt of landing hurt, but I didn't care.

Sam gave me a quizzical look. "Visit didn't go well?"

"No, it went really well actually." I started picking at my cuticles, avoiding eye contact.

"What's up then?"

"I wanna go home. I want to stay with her."

"Ah. I get it." She sounded distant.

"I know I need to be here, it just...sucks."

Sam nodded, tapping her fingers on the table. Her posture was forced, stiff. A large change from the usual loose and effortless way she carried herself. While bouncing her leg, she kept glancing around the room. I squinted, noticing her distress.

"Are you okay?"

She didn't answer me, but kept glancing around the room as if something were about to come out and attack her. She fidgeted as I leaned forward and tried to get her attention.

"Sam?"

She was shaking, and her breathing was becoming more frantic. She seemed both unaware and too aware of her surroundings at the same time. Was this what I looked like when it felt like all the air was sucked out of the room? I rested one of my hands on hers and she snapped her head up to look at me. Her eyes focused on me but I could tell she was struggling to stay present.

"I...I need meds," she muttered, but didn't get up from her seat. Maybe she couldn't?

I went and got a nurse – not the bitter one – and led her back to Sam. She knelt down in front of her and tried to get her attention.

"Do you want your Ativan?"

She managed a nod as tears welled in the corners of her eyes. The nurse left and came back a minute later with a couple small cups. Sam took them quickly. The nurse gave her a faint smile and then left. I was expecting her to stay and try and help, but found myself alone in trying to keep Sam present. I decided to try something while waiting for her meds to kick in.

Touching her hand again, I said softly, "Sam?"

She glanced at me in between her darting movements.

"What color is my shirt?"

She squinted. I could almost feel the fog that she was fighting against.

"Blue," she managed.

"How many chairs are at this table?"

"Three." The focus in her eyes became a little sharper.

"What color are my eyes?"

"Gold." She rubbed her eyes, taking in a deep breath.

Taking her shoes off, she placed her feet firmly on the floor and spread her hands out on the table. I kept asking her to name things until eventually she looked up at me, much more present.

"Look at you, learning things already." There was a smile in her tone that wasn't on her face.

I stifled a laugh before asking, "Are you okay now?"

"Better, thanks. My anxiety attacks are pretty rare, but they come out of nowhere sometimes. What happened on your visit? Give me something to focus on."

The plastic of the chair dug into me as I leaned, so I pressed my hands on the table to adjust myself before answering.

"It was really good. I told her about going by Theo. She said she liked it."

Sam offered a faint smile. "See? I told you she'd be one of the good ones."

Smiling back, I added, "she's excited for me to cut my hair...called me handsome."

"Did you like that?"

"Yeah..." I felt awkward talking about a compliment but couldn't contain the happiness that washed over me. I never knew how to handle compliments.

"I'm glad things are coming together for you. You deserve a little joy. Things can be hard and get better at the same time, you see? You've just gotta let the right people in."

Letting out a sigh, I nodded. She'd helped me so much, I didn't know how to repay her for it.

"Sam?"

"Yeah?"

"Thank you...for everything."

"You're welcome, baby queer." She snickered.

––––––––––

Moving a meeple forward, I took a card and read its instructions. Today I'd chosen Life as the game we'd pretend to play while diving into my trauma.

Carmen spun the wheel and moved her piece before asking, "What would you like to start with today?"

This time, I was ready with something I'd been thinking about for days. "How do you accept someone's love when you feel like you don't deserve it?"

"Huh." She leaned back, clearly not expecting such a straightforward question to follow her own. "That's tough. I guess we should start with why you feel like you don't deserve love in the first place."

"I dunno, I just...feel like I'm a bad person. Bad people shouldn't have the kind of love I want. I've never felt like I had it before now."

"Do you think not having it before might contribute to you feeling like a bad person that doesn't deserve love?"

Thoughts raced through my mind, flashes of times I'd had hate spewed in my direction throughout my life. A slap from a foster mother when I alluded that I might like girls. Being shunned by a family when I refused to speak their language, one I'd associated with hatred. Shouts and spit from my biological father after he'd learned of my mother's death. While blinking, I shook my head to try and ward away the onslaught of negative history.

"If you experience enough hatred as a child, positive interactions can be difficult to navigate because you never learned how. How about we start with one interaction you've had difficulty accepting lately?"

"When Alex says she loves me. I want more and it feels good, but I feel guilty at the same time."

"What do you feel guilty about?"

"She shouldn't be stuck with me. I'm not worth her love."

"Shouldn't she be the one to determine what her love is worth?"

"I guess."

"Then if she's giving it to you, that means she's decided you are worthy of love. Even though you might feel like you're not. The matter that's up to you is whether or not you accept it. Do you accept her love?"

"I want to. It's just...so hard."

"Let me ask you this, Theo. Do you have any love for yourself?"

Absolutely not.

I shrugged.

"What do you give your love to?"

"Alex...someone who deserves it."

"And has Alex done everything perfectly her whole life?"

"I guess not."

"But she still deserves your love?"

"Yes."

"Then why don't you deserve hers?"

"I just...I'm not good like her. I hurt people. I do bad shit."

Resting my chin on my knee, I sighed.

You're worthless.

"Is it things that others have told you, or things that you've done that make you feel like you're a bad person?"

"Both."

The carpet seemed like it was warping beneath me. Everything was out of touch as my ears started ringing. I still didn't understand how any of this was meant to help. My reality started slipping away, and I let it. Guilt and shame overtook me. How was anyone supposed to "work through" things so painful? Me being a bad person was solidified in the opinions of everyone who had abandoned me and every bruise I'd left on someone else in every fight. Every drop of blood I'd drawn. Every needle I'd slid beneath my skin. There was so much evidence against me, how was this woman sitting here trying to show me the good? How could anyone see any good?

Tears didn't come today. It was like I'd used them all up over the last few sessions. There was a real heaviness to me, the typical fog that consumed me was slightly clearer, but it was replaced with a sedation I'd never experienced before. It made the thoughts louder, like they'd been given a megaphone and I'd been forced to sit down and listen. Before, they'd been this nagging undertone, only coming to the surface when my emotions broke though. The emotions felt more dull, not so overwhelming. I felt flat, distant and dissonant. My thoughts continued swirling around me, like an ocean I was slowly drowning in.

Bringing my attention back to the board game, I spun the wheel. Carmen was looking at me expectantly. Shit, I'd missed a question, hadn't I? I didn't really care that much, this all felt so pointless. I continued the game as if she hadn't said anything, because I hadn't heard anything anyway.

"Theo?"

"Yeah?"

"You seem very flat today. Do you know if you're having any side effects from your medications?"

"I dunno. Everything just feels really hopeless. I don't know how any of this will help."

"I see. You haven't felt any relief over the past few days?"

"It's so up and down. Sometimes I feel a little better, but dragging this stuff up hurts and I don't like it."

"It's difficult at first, you're right. The idea is that working through this stuff helps you let it go so it doesn't weigh on you so heavily. I've noticed you engaging more which is a positive sign, but today you feel very distant. It's okay to have bad days, but I want to be sure that you're not being affected negatively by your medications."

"I feel heavy, but not like emotionally heavy. Just...it feels like I'm moving through molasses or something."

"Hm..." Carmen wrote a note on a paper next to her. "Sometimes medications can have a sedating effect. If it doesn't go away you might need a change. Just keep letting us know how you're feeling, okay?"

"Okay."

How much longer would that be? How much longer would I be stuck here?

"I want to go home."

She gave me a weak smile. "Do you feel like you're safe enough to be home?"

"I dunno, urges come and go."

"I don't think you're ready yet, personally."

Audibly sighing, I spun the wheel again even though it wasn't my turn. I needed something to do with my hands.

"How will we know when I'm ready? Not everything's just gonna stop."

"You're right, it won't, but it will get better. You'll be able to handle your emotions a little better and will have learned more tools to use when you're in distress. You've done very well so far, you're listening and trying, I can tell."

"I'm so tired. Everything is so exhausting."

"Why don't we call it here for today? You go rest."

Nodding, I got up from the floor and walked back to my room. Sam wasn't there, she must've been off doing her own thing. It was all for the best, I didn't really want to talk anyway. I ached to be with Alex. Thankfully, I'd have a visit with her later. Until then, I lay down, closing my eyes and shutting out the world.

————

Again, I awoke to Sam nudging me. "Alex is here."

Wordlessly, I got up and staggered into the common room where Alex was sitting at our table. I plopped down next to her and leaned on her shoulder, closing my eyes and breathing in her scent. She felt like home.

Alex wrapped an arm around my shoulders and kissed the top of my head, grinning her beautiful smile. I traced my fingers along the pattern on her leggings. A floral, curvy pattern. It was a struggle to keep my eyes slightly open.

"Are you okay?" The concern in her voice echoed through my head.

The words felt like they reached my ears in slow motion. It was so hard to focus.

"Tired."

"Do you want to go back and lay down? I can come back—"

"No." I wound my arms around her waist, trapping her

in the seat. "I don't...want you to leave." My words were slow and labored. Every syllable took a distinct effort to leave my mouth.

She pulled me closer and kissed the top of my head again. "I have a surprise for you when you come home. I got you something. Then I was thinking we could go out shopping and get your hair cut. Does that sound okay?"

"Yeah." I said sleepily.

Any enthusiasm I had was sapped out of me by this heavy tiredness. I wanted to be excited, but didn't have the energy for it.

Alex ran her hand through my hair. "Did you sleep last night?"

"Yeah...and most of the day..."

She squinted. 'Do they have you on meds?"

"Mhm." I closed my eyes again, letting my hands fall into her lap. I just wanted to curl up with her and sleep.

"I'll be right back."

"No..."

It was too late. She was already up, and I fell against the chair where she was sitting. She caught me before my face hit the hard plastic, and then slowly lowered my head down. My movements were so drastically slowed that I couldn't even catch myself. She brushed my hair out of my face before leaving.

She came back a couple minutes later with the cheery, round-faced nurse I'd come to know as Ginny.

"...They shouldn't be this tired, should they?" I caught the back end of Alex's sentence and while I couldn't muster up a grin on the outside, I rejoiced internally at the sound of my correct pronouns coming out of her mouth.

"Theo, can you sit up for me please?" Ginny asked with her honey-sweet tone.

I struggled to push myself up from the seat of the chair, and almost fell again when Alex caught me. While I didn't see it, I could feel the look that Alex and Ginny exchanged over me. Alex supported my weight in her arms as she helped me sit up. Ginny took my vitals and her sweet smile faded for a fraction of a second before she plastered a new, much faker one on her face.

"I'm going to talk to one of the doctors," she said, promptly leaving me and Alex alone.

Alex sat back down next to me and I rested my head in her lap. She stroked my hair while waiting and whispered to me some words that I couldn't make out. It was getting harder and harder to stay awake, but I desperately tried so that Alex could stay longer.

Ginny came back a few minutes later with a wheelchair and beckoned for me to get in it. I was resistant, or at least tried to be in my state. Alex lifted my face up in her hands and whispered to me.

"It's okay honey, I'll come back tomorrow."

"No…" I used all my strength to cling to her much like a child would cling to a parent on the first day of school.

"Theo, we're going to have you lay down and then monitor you for a bit. We think you might be reacting negatively to one of your medications." Ginny's voice was much more stern, but still had a sweet undertone.

I relented. I didn't want to, but I didn't have the strength to argue. Alex helped me into the wheelchair and then cupped my face in her hands as she kissed me on the lips.

I held on to her hands as long as I could and she whispered, "I love you" into my ear.

"I…love you…" My speech was delayed and almost sounded as if I'd been drinking.

I looked into her eyes enough to see tears brimming up in them. I hated her seeing me like this. It hurt her. She got up and walked away towards the door as Ginny wheeled me in the opposite direction. Once we were in my room again, I got out of the chair and with Ginny's help, staggered into my bed. Collapsing onto the mattress, I buried my face in the pillow as she covered me up with a blanket.

CHAPTER ELEVEN

I woke up to see Sam sitting on her bed reading. It was light out. How much time had passed? I felt a lot better – clearer. Sam looked up from her book and smiled.

"Hey there."

Rubbing my eyes and stretching, I asked, "how long was I out?"

"About a day. Don't worry, you didn't miss Alex today. We've got about an hour until visitors come."

"Fuck me."

"No thanks." She stuck her tongue out and smiled at me.

I rolled my eyes but couldn't help a stifled laugh escaping. "They're not gonna give me that shit again, are they?"

"I doubt it, they'll probably try a different medication since you reacted badly to that one. Can't promise it'll be better though. Took them years to get my shit right."

"Years?"

"Yeah, but not every med will knock you out like that, some just plain don't do anything. It's a lot of trial and error."

As if on cue, a nurse walked in. She started taking my vitals and looked at me with some concern on her face.

"How're you feeling today, Theo?"

"Better."

"Good." She continued taking my vitals, and looked satisfied as the concern melted away from her face once she finished. "The doctor's changed your medication – this one hopefully won't make you so tired." She handed me the growingly familiar set of paper cups – one with pills, one with water.

I looked at the pills briefly before popping them in my mouth. If they took years to get right, might as well try everything and get it over with. How much worse could it be? I'd been getting the best sleep of my life, at the very least.

With her job done, the nurse turned and went to leave. Her hand on the door, she quickly turned back to me. "Please let us know if you start feeling off again, okay?"

"Sure."

She then exited the room, leaving Sam and I alone.

"Sam?"

"Yeah?"

"You said your parents were supportive of you, how come they don't come and visit?"

She glanced down at her book briefly before answering. "Remember, I said they were lawyers? They both work a lot, and visiting is during when they're at the office. They come on Sundays as long as they're not working a case that has them doing overtime."

"Oh." Seemed legitimate enough. "Don't you get lonely?" I couldn't imagine being in here without the hope of Alex showing up every day.

She shrugged, her whole body bouncing with the motion.

"Sometimes. I call them every once in a while. Otherwise, I've got you and the other people here."

"I'm not much company. Been sleeping almost the whole time."

She snickered. "Well, when you're awake you're damn good at cards. I'm gonna beat you one of these times."

"Do you wanna meet Alex?"

A grin cracked across her face. "Sure!" She visibly tried to rein in her excitement, "I mean, if it wouldn't be interrupting you two."

"Interrupting what?" I wrinkled my nose. "There's people watching us like hawks. That one nurse always gets mad when we kiss or hug too much."

Sam rolled her eyes. "Karen." Making a sour face, she went on, "I swear I catch her calling me 'he' under her breath sometimes. She's a real charmer, homophobic and transphobic as fuck."

"That's fucked up."

"You're telling me. In my opinion, you guys should lay on the PDA just to piss her off." She snickered.

"Won't she make Alex leave?"

"Nah, she can't do that. Unless you guys are being absolutely disgusting, which, you don't seem like the type. Subtle shit, you know?"

"Hah...maybe." The idea sounded amusing at the very least. Pissing off homophobes can be fun when they can't retaliate.

The door creaked open a bit and the nurse from earlier called in. "Theo, you have a visitor."

I motioned for Sam to follow as I walked out into the hallway. She came with me gladly and we both sat at the table with Alex. Sam across from her, me next to her and embracing her in a tight hug. She hugged me back and then pulled away to kiss my forehead.

"Feeling better today?"

"Yeah." Smiling, I breathed in her scent. I couldn't get enough. Before I became too lost in her, I pulled myself back to reality and gestured towards Sam. "This is my friend, Sam."

Alex grinned and held out her hand for Sam to shake. She took it earnestly and smiled back. "Hey."

"Hi! Theo told me how you've been helping them with figuring out their gender and stuff. They already seem so much more comfortable, thank you so much."

Sam blushed. Alex had that effect on people.

"You know that nurse that keeps getting mad at us?" I whispered to Alex. "Sam said she's a huge homophobe and that's why."

Alex glanced around to find said nurse. "Oh, really? How about we piss her off then?"

She planted a kiss that I wasn't expecting right on my lips and held us there for a few seconds.

Sam started cackling. The happiest sound I'd ever heard her make. "I knew I'd like her."

She clapped her hands as Alex pulled away from me and shot a glare in Karen's direction. The woman turned her nose up at us and looked away, trying to make it seem like she hadn't been watching.

Alex rested her hand on my lower back. The movement came to her so naturally, I wasn't even sure if she'd intended to do it. Regardless, it sent tingles up my spine and made me want more.

She turned back to Sam with a mischievous grin. "So, what's your story?"

Sam waved a hand in the air. "You know, bipolar mess of a trans girl, nothing too wild."

"What made you take Theo under your wing?"

"I've got a pretty good sense for baby queers, and I kinda wish someone had been around to show me the ropes, you feel? If I can make it easier for someone, I want to." She shot me a sideways smile, "Plus, they're pretty endearing."

"Tell me about it." Alex moved her hand from my lower back to stroke my hair. "They hooked me when I was eleven and I haven't left since."

I looked at Alex quizzically, "What do you mean?"

"Don't tell me you don't remember. You looking like a lost puppy alone in the school cafeteria. I had to come keep you company."

I tried to stifle the grin that forced its way onto my face. Had she really noticed me like that all the way back then? Had we both had feelings for each other this whole time? How much torture had I put myself through for no reason? My smile fell away.

"What's wrong?"

"I just...wish I'd told you sooner."

"Oh honey, there's plenty of time still." She leaned in to kiss my forehead, no longer for show.

Then the thought hit me – I'd almost made sure that there wasn't. I had almost robbed us both of the experience of loving one another. I would've taken a piece of her heart with me – hurt her in a way that would almost assuredly never completely heal. It was the first time I'd truly been hit with regret for what I'd done. What if I had succeeded? I never would've known the love that I felt now. I would've died without ever knowing the sheer joy that came from her kisses, the warmth I felt when she held me.

I broke. All at once, I was sobbing and falling into Alex's arms. I really, truly, did not want to die. This was the first time in my life that I felt a sense of wanting to be alive – and it scared me.

Alex grasped my shoulders and held me at arm's length. "Hey, hey, what's going on?"

I couldn't form any words, only incoherent stutters escaped me and my breathing was so erratic that I thought I might pass out.

"Breathe, honey, it's okay."

I fell into her as she drew me into her arms. How could I be so careless? How was I willing to hurt her so badly? I was slowly realizing that people actually cared about me – that I'd be missed. People wouldn't be happy with me gone – it was all lies that my depression had told me.

I started gaining control again while Alex stroked my hair. I took a few breaths, gradually slowing down and coming back to the present. I was okay. I hadn't died. I was still here.

Thanks to her.

I slowly pulled out of Alex's embrace. "I'm okay...It's okay."

I hadn't realized, but Sam was now kneeling next to my chair as well.

"What happened?" Alex wiped the tears from my face.

"I just...I don't want to die."

My breathing had slowed and everything felt a little bit clearer. It was a clarity I couldn't remember ever experiencing before. A sense of calm washed over me.

Sam's expression shifted drastically, but it was still a positive one. One of a deep understanding no one's ever had for me before. There were tears in her eyes.

"I get it. You want to live. You've had this voice telling you you'd be better off dead for so long – you just finally realized it was lying to you."

I nodded. Then, she hugged me.

"Good job, baby queer. That's a big step."

"Everything's always felt so pointless, so unreal. It's all sharper now, like I'm actually really here for the first time."

Alex understood now. Tears welled up in her eyes to match mine, and she pulled me in for a hug. She held me tightly, taking in a deep breath, like the weight of the world had just fallen off her shoulders.

Everything wasn't suddenly fixed by any means. I still had things to work through. They weren't magically gone because I'd broken through the fog once. However, I had a faint bit of hope that one day, things wouldn't weigh on me so heavily. Hope for a future, somewhere to go in life. At least, someone to go with me. I felt good about that.

Giving Alex a genuine smile, I wiped happy tears from my eyes, and then from hers. She broke into a laugh, and I laughed with her. We became a beautiful mess of laughter and tears, not caring what we looked like.

"I fucking love you so much." I said, though fits of giggling. And then I kissed her.

It took her by surprise and she was still laughing a bit, but soon leaned into me. Her lips were so soft, and I intertwined my fingers in her hair as she cupped my face in her hands. I took in a deep breath and so did she, savoring every second. The kiss only lasted a minute, but felt like an eternity. A blissful, happy eternity.

Some disgruntled noises came from Karen's direction, but we truly did not care. I was so happy to be there, with Alex, and I never gave a fuck what anyone but her thought of me anyway. I pressed my forehead to hers and she moved her hands down to my shoulders as I continued stroking her hair. Her luscious, fiery red hair that you could see for miles. Feeling so light, I wondered if this was what it felt like to fly. I'd never felt so weightless in my life, like my feet weren't even on the cold linoleum floor.

Sam had sat back down in the chair across from us, and was now shuffling a deck of cards. Realizing she must've felt like an awkward third wheel, I turned to her with the silliest looking grin still plastered across my face.

"Sorry...I know you didn't want to feel like you were interrupting anything."

She waved a hand, her face still as bright as ever. "Don't be! You two are adorable and I'm loving how pissed off Karen is." She nodded in the direction of the nurse whose face was now three shades a darker red and twisted into an unpleasant snarl. "You're happy, it's a good change from how you've been since you got here. Don't ever be sorry for being happy."

She dealt a hand for each of us. "We're gonna play rummy though, maybe with you distracted by her I can finally win."

I chuckled and picked up my cards, "Fat chance."

———

Carmen sat in a chair across from me. We didn't bother with the ruse of a board game today, I actually wanted to talk.

"How're you doing today, Theo?"

My silly grin hadn't left even though Alex had.

"Good. Really good."

"That's great. Do you want to tell me about it?"

"Everything feels calmer, it's so much easier for me to think and feel things. Stuff's not so heavy."

"Are you having any of the side effects you were feeling the other day?"

"No."

"That's really good. I hate to kill your mood, but since you're feeling so much better, do you think we could try diving into some hard stuff today?"

I felt ready. Not that anything we'd talked about before wasn't hard.

"Okay."

"What led you to your actions that brought you here?"

"You mean, why did I try to kill myself?"

"Essentially, yes. In order to make sure you're safe enough to go home, we've got to find ways for you to deal with the circumstances that challenge you the most."

"I...hurt someone. Really bad. I got arrested. And then the officer brought out my file and started digging stuff up. Mom was upset with me. I felt like I just fucked everything up. I didn't want to hurt people anymore."

"So you felt like killing yourself would stop you from hurting people?"

"Yes."

"You didn't think that the act of killing yourself would hurt anyone else?"

"No. I felt like they'd be happier if I was gone. I know that's not true now, it just kinda hit me yesterday how much it would hurt people."

"Who would it hurt?"

"Alex. It would hurt Alex. Probably my mom – she'd feel responsible. Maybe my brother. And Jeremy, my friend."

"If you were to be in the same position again, what would you do now?"

"I'd try to do better. Maybe talk to someone about what was hurting me, or how I could avoid hurting someone else."

"That's a really good idea. How do you know you hurt someone else then, when you didn't talk to them before?"

"I beat a kid up, sent him to the hospital. Alex was there, and I could hear her crying."

"So you physically hurt someone – what made you feel like that was the best option?"

"He spanked me, and I just lost control. It's happened a few times, I don't give a shit what people say to me but when someone touches me I just react and don't think. I get so angry."

"Where do you think this anger comes from?"

"Touch has never been good for me. Not before Alex."

"I know you mentioned your birth father being abusive – do you think some of it might stem from that?"

"Yeah...and other stuff…"

"Other people hurt you too?"

"Yeah…"

"Were you ever sexually abused, or only physically?"

My stomach dropped. Good feeling gone. I didn't answer her, but instead started fidgeting with my hands, wishing we'd brought out a board game after all. I looked down at my lap as my face grew hotter.

Carmen gathered everything she needed from my reaction.

"Is it happening now?"

"No," I muttered, grabbing a pillow off the couch I was sitting on and held it to my chest.

"Did you ever tell anyone?"

"No."

"Theo, that's big. I think anyone with that kind of trauma would react negatively when touched if they didn't want it."

Tears welled up in my eyes and I squeezed the pillow tightly, putting all my strength into the pressure.

"Can you tell me who it was?"

"I don't want to talk about this."

I wanted to shut down. As it was, I was fighting against the fog that I'd rid myself of the day before. It was trying to come back. I didn't want it. I wanted that lightness to stay with me, it was so intoxicating. Would it ever come back?

"How old were you?" Carmen tried to ignore the wall I'd put up.

"I *said,* I don't want to talk about this." There was an edge of anger in my tone.

Leave me alone.

"Okay, that's okay. How about we go back to what happened on the day you hurt someone? You said Alex was crying, did you feel like you hurt her too?"

"Yes."

"What upset you the most about that?"

"It makes me feel like I'm like my father. I never want to hurt her like that."

"Do you worry about that a lot? Being like your father?"

"Yeah. I scare myself when I get really angry."

"Have there ever been times where you were able to pull yourself out of an anger like that?"

"Yeah. I usually can when Alex is around. I don't want her to see it."

"Does she talk you down, or do you usually regulate yourself better when she's there?"

"I guess I get myself to calm down. I remind myself that she's there and it's a little easier to not get so angry."

"Would you be interested in learning some techniques to calm yourself when she's not around?"

"Okay."

"Okay, so first we start with identifying triggers. What specific things can you think of that make you angry?"

"When people touch me and I don't want them to. When people are hurting others." I paused for a second, thinking, "When people bring up my past."

"What helps you stay calm?"

"Alex...I don't really know what else."

"Have you ever tried taking a few deep breaths before acting?"

"No. I've never thought to."

"I've noticed breathing techniques have been helpful for you when you get upset here. What do you think about maybe trying them when you get angry?"

"I can try."

"There was a bit of anger in you when I pressed for information. How did you calm yourself from that?"

"You stopped before I got really mad. And I like you, so it's easier to not get mad."

"Say I kept pressing, what do you think you would have done?"

"Probably walked out."

"See, that's a non-violent reaction and perfectly acceptable. You have the right to walk away when someone's making you upset. I believe you might have a better handle on your anger than you think."

"It's easier to handle with people I like. I don't know what to do when it's someone I don't like and I lose control. It's scary when that happens."

"I think we're all guilty of losing control sometimes, that doesn't mean you're like your father. Everyone has some degree of anger in them. I think you have every right to be angry, especially in the situations you've described. What you do with the anger is what's important. It sounds like most of the time you handle it appropriately, so how do you think we can carry that over into times when it's someone you don't like causing the anger?"

"I don't know. It's like all the anger I don't use on people I like gets pent up and then when someone threatens me it all comes over me at once and I can't stop it."

"I see. Maybe we need to find an outlet for your anger before it gets built up like that. What kind of activities make you feel good?"

"Skating...and sometimes writing."

"Writing is a really good skill to have – do you think you might be able to express your anger there? Have you ever tried it?"

"I haven't tried. I guess I could."

"I think that's a good thing to practice. Maybe you could keep a journal?"

"I guess. I could write about other stuff too, as long as no one reads it."

"That's a really good idea. For now, why don't I give you a few sheets of paper you could use? You don't have to show them to me after, but feel free to if you decide that's what you want."

"Okay."

Carmen went to her desk and pulled out some loose-leaf lined paper. She handed it to me with a smile.

"I want that to be your homework, okay? Fill up a page or two, then rip them up, throw them away, do whatever you want with them. All I want you to tell me next time is how you felt afterwards."

Taking the paper, I nodded at her. My grip on the pillow had loosened considerably, and I set it to the side.

"You did a good job today, Theo. I'm seeing a lot of progress in you. I think you might be ready to go home soon."

She showed me to the door, and I walked out into the hallway with the papers in hand. I didn't feel as groggy as I had after previous sessions, it wasn't as hard today. Maybe things really were getting better. This was helping, as much as I'd doubted it before.

Looking at the clock, I realized that this was the first time I'd actually made it through the whole session. She'd let me go early every other time because I got so overwhelmed. A slight sense of pride grew in me, flickering out of the darkness.

I'm getting better. I can actually do this.

A grin gradually grew across my face, that light feeling returning to me. It was back! It wasn't a fluke, I was actually able to feel *good*.

CHAPTER TWELVE

The smell of cigarette smoke and alcohol filled the air. I crept silently towards the exit. He didn't see me, thankfully. Creating an ungodly squeak, the door creaked open as I pushed it, alerting him to my presence. An incoherent yell came from the kitchen, and I bolted the rest of the way out the door.

I ran as fast as my tiny legs could carry me. He wouldn't catch me. No, he was too far gone in his drunken stupor to catch a five-year-old who was accustomed to running away from danger. Running away from *him*. I ran all the way into the woods, until I was out of breath and out of sight of the house. If you could call that run-down hellhole a house. He looked after the place even less than he looked after me.

Taking in a deep breath, I smelled the damp earth beneath my feet. It had recently rained, which is why I'd been inside in the first place. I always tried to be away as much as I could. I loved the smell of the woods – it carried an air of safety for me. He never followed me in here. He was always too intoxicated, too clumsy not to trip over every root that stuck its way into the path I effortlessly followed. I'd practically lived in these woods.

At least since mom was gone.

A part of me still ached when I thought of her. It had only been a year since she died, still fresh in my memory. I missed her calming presence, her kisses, the love she was always sure to tell me that she felt. She was nothing like my father.

He didn't deserve her.

But he was a better man with her. He still had his temper, but it was far more subdued and he would never raise a hand to her. No, the drinking started after she was gone. It was like a whole new monster was born from the shell of a man that was left behind. A monster that hated me. Hated how similar I was to her. Hated seeing her face in mine.

Since I was staring down at my feet, I walked straight into a man that appeared in my path. Looking up, my stomach dropped. I knew this man, even though I hadn't met him yet. He wasn't my father, but a father figure in a family I'd come to stay with years later. Tall, muscular, and thick, he looked over me.

"Elizabeth, you're so beautiful."

A scream died on my lips as I woke up. My skin crawled. I felt so dirty. I got up and ran into the bathroom, not even looking to see if I'd woken Sam up. Scrambling, I turned the water for the shower on and started tearing off my clothes in a frenzy. I made the water close to scalding and got in, feverishly scrubbing myself with soap and a washcloth. Breathing was so hard that I took gasping, panicked breaths in between practically trying to scrub my skin off. I sank to the floor of the shower and started crying, water adding to the tears that were streaming down my face.

There was a knock on the door.

"Theo? You okay?"

No. No I was not. But I couldn't answer.

My sobbing must've been loud enough that she could hear me, because she went on, "Do you need anything?"

She was quiet as I tried to stifle my sobs. Why couldn't I just sleep without ghosts haunting me? That was the only reason I'd liked the drug-induced sleep I'd been getting before – there weren't any nightmares. I could be at peace. My normal brain would never let me do that. There was too much it felt the need to remind me of, especially when it had been brought up the day prior. It was as if my brain was happy to add to the torture I'd experienced throughout my life – did I secretly think I deserved it? Why was I forced to relive things over and over?

My sobs slowed and my now incredibly irritated skin was enough incentive to leave the cocoon of the shower. The steam in the bathroom was thick as I groped around and realized I'd forgotten to get clothes in my frenzy. I knocked on the door.

"S-Sam?"

"Yeah?" She was still right next to the door. She'd waited until I was ready.

"Could...could you grab me some clothes?"

"Sure."

A moment later, she knocked on the door and I cracked it enough for her to pass the clothes through.

"Thanks."

She went back to her bed, and I started getting dressed. She'd given me a comfy set of pajamas that I slid into. Once I was dressed, I took a deep breath and opened the door.

The air felt cold compared to the steam of the bathroom. It would have been refreshing, had I not still felt so disgusting. I sat down on the floor next to my bed, not wanting anything to do with sleep.

Fuck this. Fuck him. Fuck them both. Why can't they just leave me alone?

Sitting, I stared at the wall as thoughts began to overtake me. Memories, emotions, everything I didn't want to deal with. Before I was too far gone, I decided to try what Carmen had told me. I grabbed the paper and a pen from the table next to my bed and furiously started scribbling everything that came into my mind.

How could you do that to me? You're a monster, a pervert, praying on a defenseless child that begged you to stop. You gained my trust and then used it against me, breaking it into a million pieces and leaving me helpless to trust anyone ever again. I was a child. A CHILD. I'd already been hurt, and you decided to capitalize on that and destroy me completely. You're the reason for my first suicide attempt, when I went back into the system after the first good home I had I was terrified I'd end up in the hands of someone like you again. I'd rather choose death than live through what you did to me. You made me feel so worthless and disgusting. I know now you're the one that's worthless, but somehow you can still make me feel like I'm that little kid that couldn't fight back. You still haunt me.

And YOU. You were supposed to take care of me. Instead, you ensured that every childhood memory was tainted with fear. And then you blamed me for your actions. Somehow it was always something I did that made you hit me. I was too needy. I was in the way. I think we both know the truth was that I reminded you of mom, and you couldn't handle that. It wasn't my fault. It was yours.

I pressed so hard on the pen that it ripped the paper. Tears were falling onto the page as I took it into my hands and in one swift motion ripped it in half.

And again.

And again.

I tore the page until there was nothing left to rip, and there was just a small pile of paper in front of me. I wished I could light it on fire, but I didn't exactly have access to a lighter or matches in here. So I did the next best thing. I took every little piece of paper and flushed it down the toilet. Watching as the last few pieces slid down in the current of water, my hands shook. I took a deep breath, held it, and then let it out. Then, I fell to the floor. My legs were weak and couldn't hold me up any longer.

But inside, I felt a little better. I didn't feel the need to scrub my skin off anymore, and I felt a little less pressure inside myself. Sitting on the floor for a minute, those thoughts that I'd written were cleared away to make room for me to try and think of things that made me happy. I thought about Alex, and how if she'd been there she would've held me until I felt better. Longing for her touch, I rubbed my still irritated arms.

Getting up, I walked out of the bathroom and sat on my bed. I sighed, and then looked over at Sam, who was now wide awake and reading her book by the light coming in from the window.

She looked up at me, "You okay now?"

"I...I think so."

"You should ask for something for your nightmares, you know there's meds that help with them?"

"Really?" That sounded *amazing*. Sleeping without the constant threat of bad memories.

"Yeah. Talk to the doctors tomorrow."

"Sorry I woke you up."

"S'alright. You owe me a game now though."

I gave her a half smile. "Sure."

———

I decided on a game of rummy with Carmen – realizing I needed something to do with my hands while talking, but knowing the game didn't really matter. I dealt out the cards before asking.

"Sam told me there's meds for nightmares. Do you think I could try some?"

"I know you had that one really bad one since you've been here – are they really common for you?"

"I have them almost every night. I had another one last night, that's why she suggested it."

"Are you ever reluctant to go to sleep because of them?"

"All the time. When I was using I'd do it before bed so that I wouldn't dream."

"Okay. That's definitely something we can look into. I'll talk to the psychiatrist on your case and see if we can maybe add something for them. Does that sound okay?"

"Yeah."

"Now my question for you – did you do that homework we talked about?"

"Yeah, I wrote last night after my nightmare."

"What did you do with it? How did you feel afterwards?"

"I ripped it up and flushed it down the toilet. I felt a little better after."

"Good! Good, I'm glad it helped. Would you be willing to do it again if you needed an outlet?"

"I think so. It helped with the thoughts that usually end up screaming in my head when I don't feel good."

She smiled. "Do you feel like you're almost ready to leave?"

"I don't know what ready looks like, but I do feel better."

"I think you're just about there. We'll need to set you up with an outpatient therapist and psychiatrist for follow up, but I think you'll do well with that."

"Really?" My heart fluttered. I wanted to go home more

than anything.

"Absolutely. You've learned a lot of skills since you've been here and have been working very hard on using them. I think with a good support system, things will keep getting better for you. We'll see about that med change and you can probably go tomorrow or the day after."

Grinning, I stifled a squeak of joy. I couldn't wait to be with Alex. Hold her without looming eyes watching us. What I wasn't looking forward to – getting a new therapist. I trusted Carmen in a way that didn't come to me easily, and I wasn't sure how hard it would be for me to find that with a new therapist.

"Could I just keep seeing you?"

"Unfortunately no, I only work on the inpatient unit. I don't see people outside of here. Don't worry though, I have someone in mind for you. I think you'll like her."

"Okay."

Sam. I was gonna miss Sam. I had to tell her I was leaving. How had I beaten her out? I'd only been here a couple weeks. I never thought I'd be reluctant to leave.

"What if I fuck it up?"

"If you need to, you can always come back. It's normal to be a little apprehensive about leaving. You'll be okay."

"It's weird, all I've wanted to do since I got here is leave, but now that I can I'm nervous."

"That's pretty common. You get used to how things are here – the support, the people – it's almost nerve-wracking to go home where it's different. We're going to make sure you still have all the support you need there, so you won't be alone when you go."

"Okay." I laid down my last card, winning the game.

With a chuckle, Carmen said "undefeated. Now, I know you want to tell Sam. Go ahead."

I nodded and left the room to go find my friend. I found her in our room, nose in a book, as usual. Walking right up to her bed, I sat down on the edge.

"Guess what?"

She lowered the book to look at me.

"Carmen said I can go home in a day or two."

"That's great!" There was a genuine happiness in her tone, but an edge of apprehension at the same time.

"I want your number. I wanna stay friends outside of here. Is that okay?"

She smiled, apprehension melting away. "Heck yes."

I grabbed her a pen and a piece of paper from the table by my bed, and she scrawled her number down and handed them back to me.

"I can't wait to see you outside of here."

CHAPTER THIRTEEN

Alex greeted me at the door as I carried my small bag of belongings towards the exit. I gave Sam a hug goodbye, and she waved me off.

"Go. Go be with your girl." Her smile was genuine despite a lilt of sadness. "I'll text you when I'm out."

"You better." I smiled back at her.

Alex pulled me out the door, waving at Sam as we left. Giggling, I wrapped my free arm around her waist and walked with her to where Mom was waiting in the car. I was out, I was free. This place had helped me immensely, but I was so happy to be going home with Alex, finally.

It was an uneventful ride home. Alex and I both sat in the back and I rested my head on her shoulder as she stroked my hair. When we got home, she led me up the stairs to my room.

"Remember that surprise I said I had for you?"

I'd completely forgotten. Now I was curious as I followed her into my room and she picked a small package up off my bed.

"Open it." Her grin was radiant.

Carefully, I opened the package to reveal what looked like

a black tank top. I looked up at her questioningly.

"What is it?"

"It's a binder! It squishes your chest down to make it look flat. You've always worn oversized shirts to hide your chest, I thought maybe you'd want to try this."

My eyes widened as I unfolded the piece of elastic fabric. I'd had no idea there was such a thing until Sam had told me. Wasting no time, I turned and ran into the bathroom and tore off my shirt and bra. Without looking in the mirror, I pulled the binder over my head. It was a bit difficult at first, the fabric bunching up around my collarbone. Eventually, I managed to pull it down and adjust it to where everything felt a little more comfortable.

Then I looked in the mirror.

I froze. Tears welled up in my eyes as a yelp escaped me. There was a knock on the door.

"Are you okay?" Her sweet voice like music.

I opened the door, unable to fix my face before doing so.

"Oh. My. God!"

Her smile reflected the way my heart felt inside as I couldn't help but hop in place a couple times. She hopped with me, placing her hands on my shoulders. It was so corny, but I didn't care. We stopped after a minute and I looked in the mirror again, running my hands down my chest to feel that it was truly flat. Turning to the side, I admired the streamlined silhouette.

Embracing Alex, I whispered in her ear, "thank you."

She bent down to pick up my t-shirt that was strewn on the floor and pulled it over my head. "Let's see how it looks with a shirt on!"

I threaded my arms through the appropriate holes and then squealed all over again as I saw my reflection. It was so flat, you could barely tell I had breasts. My usually cumbersome D cups had been reduced to what could be considered overly developed pecs. At that moment, I truly knew I wasn't a girl. Shedding myself of all the markers I'd previously had of "girl" felt *so* good. I'd never wear a bra again.

Alex picked up my hair and pulled it back away from my face. "This goes next. Let's pick out a hairstyle you like and then we can go get it cut today." She walked back into my room, but I lingered in the mirror, still enamored with how sleek I looked. It was such a rush of euphoria, no high could compare to this. I never wanted to look away.

A part of me wished that I'd known what Sam had introduced me to sooner, wondered how much better I might've felt if I had. How much of my misery was caused by living as the wrong gender? I wasn't sure, as there were obviously other things going on at the same time. But if I felt *this* good over something as small as a binder, how much better could I have been feeling? Maybe things would have been more manageable. I was a little angry over the time lost. However, I was even happier over what was to come.

I walked into my room where Alex was already sitting on my bed, looking things up on her phone. She looked up and waved me over.

"Come here! Look."

I sat down next to her and squinted at her phone before adjusting my glasses. She handed me her phone so I could look closer and leaned on me to scroll down slowly. Her touch felt so good, and I rested my head on hers.

On the screen, there were a bunch of short hairstyles ranging from buzz cuts to pixie cuts. We scrolled for a while,

Alex occasionally looking up at me as if trying to imagine the cut on my hair. It felt a little daunting, immediately going so short without trying something mid-length first, but I knew I wanted it. Eventually, I stopped on one.

"Hold on." I said, batting her hand away and tapping for a bigger picture.

Grinning, I knew it was the one. It was a short fauxhawk, the sides very gradually faded out at the neckline. The top was a bit longer, the hair flared upwards in soft spikes. Alex snatched it out of my hand, stared at it, and then looked at me.

"Oh, *fuck yes.*"

I didn't have time to laugh at her, as she was already throwing on a hoodie and dragging me up off the bed. I barely had the chance to grab my wallet on the way out. Well, Sam was right, Alex was *all about* this makeover. We almost tumbled down the stairs, we were going so fast.

Mom looked at us quizzically from the kitchen and Alex answered with, "We'regoingtothemallokseeyoulaterbye." that sounded like every word spilled out of her mouth at the same time.

I gave Mom a reassuring look as Alex hauled me out the door. Once we were out the door she slowed down, but only a little so that we could keep up the pace on the way to the mall. At least now it felt more like we were holding hands and walking instead of her dragging me like a dog on a leash.

We walked side by side, holding hands. I felt exposed, hand-holding being a sign of more than friendship at our age. Then again, being in a relationship with Alex was part of my life that I felt the least amount of shame for. I was proud that someone like her loved me. Who cares about some bigots on the street? She was my girlfriend and I wanted to shout it from the rooftops.

It was about a ten-minute walk to the mall, and it was still early enough that there was very little traffic inside. We made our way to a hair salon on the far end. It was empty, save for the receptionist and a few stylists. Alex pulled me up to the desk and the lady gave us a warm smile.

"What can we do for you today?"

"They need a cut." Alex gestured towards me.

"Okay, we can do that." The receptionist waved over a stylist.

She looked to be about in her thirties and was covered in black-and-gray tattoos. Her hair was short and bleached to a snowy white.

"What are you lookin' to do today?" She greeted us with a pleasant attitude.

"This." Alex held up her phone still open on the picture I'd selected.

The stylist's expression didn't change as she looked down at the phone and then up at me. I shifted uncomfortably under her gaze. Why did I care so much what this stylist thought of the cut I wanted?

"What's your name, hun?" Her soft southern accent told me she wasn't born and raised in the city.

"Theo."

"Anyone tried to talk you out of it?"

I swallowed a lump in my throat. I was suddenly incredibly anxious about the whole situation.

"She's the only one I've told." I sputtered, gesturing towards Alex. I couldn't figure out of the stylist was judging me or if she was just curious.

She took a few steps closer and pulled my hair back out of my face, and in one phrase, eased my anxieties.

"Good. You've got an amazing bone structure. All this hair covering it up is a crime."

I released the tension in my body, exhaling a breath that I hadn't realized I was holding. We followed her to a chair by a sink and I sat down, Alex leaning on the chair next to me. She had a giddy look on her face, seeming even more excited than I was.

The stylist set to work washing my hair, taking its length in her hands and wetting it. I hated the feeling of lying back in the chair with someone looming over me, and started fidgeting with my hands. A warm touch came over them and I glanced up to see Alex engulf my hands in her own.

The stylist smiled. "You don't gotta be nervous, hun. It's gonna be a big change but I bet you'll love it in the end."

I gave her a weak smile and tried to focus on Alex's soothing touch. Some people said getting your hair washed at a salon was relaxing. I begged to differ. Lying back with your neck exposed in a space filled with sharp objects is anything but relaxing. Thankfully, it was over and I was upright soon enough.

I sat in a chair in front of a mirror as the stylist pulled the smock over me. I squinted at my reflection, hated bangs and all, until Alex pulled my glasses off. She ran her finger down the bridge of my nose afterwards.

"Ready?"

"Yeah." I sighed, excited to lose this overbearing cloak of hair.

Taking my still-damp hair in her hands, the stylist pulled the length back into a low ponytail. Then she pulled a pair of scissors out of the drawer and said, "this is the best part."

She chopped though the hair with the most freeing sound I'd ever heard. While I couldn't see much without my glasses, I saw her dangle a dark blur of hair next to my head and then drop it to the ground. I couldn't stop the grin from overtaking my face.

"And now we make it pretty. Could I see that picture again, darlin'?"

Alex pulled out her phone again and showed the woman, who took the phone and brought it close to her face. Handing it back to Alex, she got to work. There was snipping, clipping, and some buzzing as she tilted my head in various directions to make sure everything was even. Out came the gel as she started running her hands through what little hair was left and styled it. Then, Alex put my glasses back on and stepped out of the way of the mirror so I could see.

My jaw dropped. I leaned forward, running my hands through my hair to feel if it was real. It was *amazing*. The longer hair on top of my hair curled slightly now that it wasn't so weighted down, and it spiked upwards from the styling. The sides were about an inch long and felt fuzzy as I ran my hands over them. It made my sleek jawline stand out and I could now see my ears with all their piercings.

I glanced over at Alex, who had an incredible smile plastered across her face and her hands clasped in front of her.

"Do you love it?"

Nodding vigorously, I reached out and hugged her as I laughed.

"Thank you," I said, turning to the stylist.

She smiled and handed me a business card.

"Now don't let anyone else touch it. That's my masterpiece."

I took the card and handed her a tip, paying the rest of the amount at the front desk. As soon as we got out of the shop, Alex spun me to face her and took my face in her hands.

"You're just so damn *cute*." She planted a kiss on my lips before I could react.

I kissed her back, savoring the taste of her lip gloss. She ran her hands through my freshly cut hair, and oh, it felt so good. We got a few glances from other people in the mall, and while I noticed, I didn't care.

"Come on." She took my hand and led me forward. "Let's get you some clothes."

I walked with her into a clothing store, completely unsure of myself. What did I even like? I'd been shopping on the fringes of the girl's section for years, always picking out the least feminine option without realizing it. I'd never dared to venture into the boy's section. How much different would it even be? Clothes are clothes, I never understood why they had to be arbitrarily gendered, why there was a stigma to walking into the "wrong" section, yet I'd abided by it my whole life.

Following Alex into the men's section, I rifled through some jeans. They didn't look much different than the ones I already owned, but the sizes were completely different. I was confounded by the small looking size twenty-sixes, when I was a six in women's. Alex looked over at me and upon seeing my confusion, took the pants and held them up to my waist.

"In men's, the sizes go by the inches in the waistline. It honestly makes a lot more sense than women's sizes, which feel like someone just threw a dart at a board with numbers on it and change depending on the brand."

"Oh…" I muttered, looking down at the pants that ran well past my feet when she held them up to me. "They're so long."

"Yeah…you might have to stick to women's pants, these look like they're too small for your hips too. It won't hurt to try them on if you want to, though."

Curse my anatomy. I've always had pretty wide hips, regardless of how thin the rest of me was. There was no changing bone structure, I supposed. At least the pants didn't look too different, I guessed I could find some that complemented whatever style I decided on in the women's section.

We walked into where the shirts were, and I was suddenly overwhelmed. Instead of there being maybe one rack of clothes that I gravitated towards, the whole section opened itself up to me. All the clothes seemed so much more substantial, they weren't thin and wispy like the materials I hated that overtook the women's section. The material all felt thicker, more robust. I didn't know where to start. Long sleeves? Short sleeves? Button downs?

Alex caught my deer-in-headlights look and laughed. "Have you really never even looked in the men's section?"

I shook my head, rifling through a rack of hoodies. They were all pull-over instead of the zippered ones I'd been indifferent to from the women's section. They had dragons on them. Dragons! I grinned as I pulled out a small (which still looked pretty big to me) with a blue dragon all across the front. Why were men's clothes so much cooler? This was the first time I didn't absolutely hate clothes shopping.

I hadn't realized that Alex had left me to my own devices and gone off into a different part of the store until she came back with some t-shirts and held them up to me. Freezing in place, I let her look me up and down before she turned the shirts so that I could see them.

"Do you like these?"

She knew me too well. One had a koi that looked like mine and I reached for it and took it out of her hands. The others had various patterns of birds, trees, and dragons similar to the ones of the hoodie I'd picked out.

"Yeah." I reached my arm out and showed her the hoodie I'd found.

"Ooh, that's cute!"

Next thing I knew, she guided me farther into the men's section. Underwear.

"Alex…" I blushed.

"What? I know damn well you hate panties." She winked at me.

"Shut up!" I exclaimed, a little too loud. I glanced around to see if anyone was looking.

"Here, we'll just get one of each style and then you can decide what kind you like and we can get more of it next time." She rifled through the garments as if buying men's underwear came naturally to her.

I kept glancing around and moved closer to her, and in a hushed tone admitted, "I like the ones with the dinosaurs."

She giggled and pulled a pair of boxer briefs covered in various types of dinosaurs off the rack and handed them to me. I scrambled to hide them under the shirts I already had in my arms. She picked me out a couple different styles and I hid them in a similar fashion.

"Shoes!" she said in a cheery tone.

I was happy to get out of the underwear section and followed her closely. We went to the shoes section, and everything looked enormous for my tiny women's size six feet. Alex compared a couple of the pairs to mine and frowned.

"We might have to get kids' for you instead."

It was okay, I liked the kids' shoes better anyway. There were various designs and patterns. I even found a pair of tennis shoes with koi on them and grabbed them faster than anyone could notice to try them on. They fit perfectly and I loved them. Grinning up at Alex, I lifted one foot up in the air.

She smiled at me. "C'mon, let's go try everything on."

Changing rooms presented a whole new dilemma. Should I go in the men's or women's? I stopped and stared at the signs as Alex continued to walk towards the women's section out of habit. She turned around when she realized I'd stopped, and looked at me quizzically for a second before realizing what the problem was.

"Oh. Hm," she said, standing beside me and looking at the signs with a similar disdain. There wasn't even a family changing room that I could sneak into to avoid the issue.

"I guess...I dunno. Rock, paper, scissors? I win, women's, you win, men's?"

She won. I held my breath as we walked into the changing rooms, already feeling like an impostor. Luckily, the store was pretty quiet and there was no one inside. I went into one of the stalls and set the pile of clothing I had on a chair in front of a large, full-length mirror.

First, the pants. I pulled my pair of jeans off and took out the first pair I'd picked out. I tried my damndest to get them on, but they got stuck right where my hips started to curve outwards. I couldn't even get them to my waist, there was no hope of them buttoning. When I tried to pull them up, I could feel my hip bones moving unnaturally. I'd grabbed a size up just in case, and while I was able to get them up to my waist, they were still tight around my hips and the length went well past my feet. No, I guessed I'd have to stick with women's jeans. I'd grabbed a couple of boot-cut pairs from the women's section – I couldn't tell any real visual difference between those and the men's jeans, and they fit a lot more comfortably.

I tried on the koi shirt and then stood in front of the mirror with the ensemble. With the binder, my chest looked so flat and I was no longer buying bulky sweatshirts to hide it. Everything looked so sleek, and I grinned as I looked at myself in the mirror. I barely recognized myself, and at the same time, recognized myself like I never had before. Catching a glance in the mirror didn't hurt or make me want to look away for once.

Pulling back the curtain, I looked at Alex with the biggest expression of relief. Her face lit up. She walked up close to me and pulled me to her hips by the belt loops on my pants.

"Does this feel better?" she asked, looking deep in my eyes.

"So much."

Then she turned me around and pushed me back towards the stall. "Go! Try more!" There was a grin in her tone.

I went through the rest of the clothes, keeping most of them. I put back the couple of pairs of pants that hadn't fit and we walked to the register together. I placed the pile on the counter.

The cashier looked bored, but plastered on a fake smile as we approached. "Find everything okay today, sir?"

Sir?

My heart jumped. It was different, but I didn't love it. Was a haircut and a binder enough to make me look like a boy to people? I still liked it better than miss.

The cashier did a double take and looked me over again "Er…sorry, miss."

Damn it.

I nodded and pushed the clothes forward so that he could reach them. When he got to the underwear, he glanced up at me and I blushed again, avoiding eye contact. At least he didn't comment. I paid and then he handed over two bags of clothing, waving us goodbye.

We got out of the store and Alex whispered to me, "he couldn't tell. He couldn't decide if you were a boy or a girl, because you're not."

I laughed. He did look confused.

Good.

CHAPTER FOURTEEN

When we got home, I was exhausted. Between getting discharged from the hospital, cutting my hair, and shopping, I was beyond spent. Once we were in my room, I dropped the bags of clothes and flopped onto my bed face down, not even caring that my glasses were pressing into my face. Alex set to folding the clothes and putting them away for me and I muttered a "thank you" into the mattress.

Afterwards, she sat down next to me and started rubbing circles into my back. "You okay?"

"Yeah," I turned over to look up at her, "just tired."

When I rolled over, I caught a glimpse of prescription bottles sitting on my desk. Three of them. Mom must've picked them up while we were out – they were the same meds I'd been taking in the hospital. I got up to look at them, sitting down in my desk chair. I'd been given my morning doses before leaving the hospital, but truth be told I really hadn't been keeping track of what I was on or when I was supposed to take it. They'd changed things around so many times. Thankfully, there weren't any midday doses. Only morning and night. I took the bottles and put them on one of the shelves lining my bed so that I'd see them when I woke up and went to bed. Then, I lowered myself back down on the mattress, laying my head in Alex's lap.

She stroked my hair. "Why don't we watch a movie or do something chill?"

"Okay." I grabbed my laptop and slid the desk chair over next to my bed and put something on.

I lay back down and Alex wrapped her arms around my waist, kissing the back of my neck. It sent shivers down my spine as I put my hands over hers. This. This is exactly what I'd wanted the whole time I'd been in the hospital. Just existing with her. I let out a sigh and pulled my glasses off. I didn't care that I couldn't see the movie. I let its sound and Alex's touch lull me to sleep.

I awoke maybe halfway through the movie and rolled over to see Alex sleeping next to me. Her face was so soft, so perfect, with her expression resting on a slight smile. Tucking her hair back out of her face, I kissed her on the lips. I couldn't help it. Her eyes opened slightly and I felt her smile beneath my lips as she kissed me back. She wound her arms around my shoulders and pulled me down. I let her. I landed on her chest, but didn't waver from the kiss. After a few minutes, we let our heads separate and Alex ran her hands through my hair.

Her smile reached her eyes as she whispered to me, "I love you."

"I love you too," I whispered back, the words electrifying everything down to my fingertips.

I rested my hands on her cheeks and went in for another kiss. Her hands travelled down my back, and all at once she started pulling at my shirt.

"No." I said while abruptly pulling away. It came out as a bark and seemed to startle her a bit, but her face softened quickly.

"Okay. It's okay." She sat up and reached for my face again, kissing me on the forehead. "I'm sorry."

"No, don't...don't be sorry. I don't know why I reacted like that." My heart was racing. I took in a deep breath to try and calm my body down.

"That's okay. We can wait as long as you need if you're not ready. There's no rush."

I thought she'd be angry – I knew she probably wanted it more than anything. How could she be so patient? I was more than a little frustrated with myself, how was she not frustrated with me?

You'll ruin everything. You can never make her happy.

She could see the wheels turning in my head, and brushed a stray curl up off my forehead. "Why don't we go do something else? Are you hungry?"

I wasn't really, but I heard her stomach growl at the mention of food, so I went along with it. "Sure."

We got up and staggered down the stairs, sleep still present in our limbs. Seth was in the kitchen. Apparently, we'd slept long enough for him to get home. He was in a zone, humming as he cooked what smelled like stir fry. He turned around with a pan in hand and nearly dropped it when he looked up at us.

"Holy shit. Liz—I, uh...hair."

He set the pan on the counter so that dinner wouldn't belong to the floor and then walked closer, looking me up and down. I realized I hadn't seen him since I'd been in the hospital – he didn't know I was Theo. He'd been expecting a girl with overbearing, long hair and a D cup. Instead he'd been met with mostly flat-chested me, my hair now buzzed in the back and in spikes off my forehead. I'd just come out without actually meaning to.

My reaction was an empty, hollow laugh. More like a cackle. I hadn't even had the chance to worry about what he would think, it hadn't occurred to me. I had been lost in the whirlwind of a transition that Alex led me through and hadn't thought about anyone but her. Sure, I'd thought about coming out to Seth, but it hadn't crossed my mind that my appearance would give me away.

The smirk on Alex's face told me that she was going to force me to handle this one on my own. Seth was still staring at me in bewilderment, he was trying not to make it look obvious that he was stealing confused glances at my chest.

"It's...it's Theo now."

"Okay, uh, please tell me you told her?"

Alex answered that question for him by wrapping her arms around my waist and kissing me on the neck.

Seth loosened up at that sight. "Phew, if you'd told me she still didn't know after all this I might have to slap you. So you're...a boy?"

"No…" I fidgeted with my hands and then rested them on the counter in front of him. "But I'm not a girl either. I use they/them."

He nodded his head, picking the pan back up and stirring it with a wooden spoon. "Okay, Theo, can you grab some plates? We can talk more when we've got food."

Glad he wasn't making a big deal of it, I grabbed some plates out of the cupboard and laid them down on the counter as Seth filled them with stir fry. Alex grabbed forks for everyone and started digging in before I even sat down.

Seth pulled up a stool for himself on the other side of the counter. "Glad someone always appreciates my cooking."

Alex laughed through a mouthful, nodding her head.

I picked at my food and pushed it around the plate without really eating anything. It looked good, but after realizing I hadn't told Seth anything I remembered I hadn't told Mom either. How would she react? How did Seth feel about it?

"So...you're okay with it?" I managed.

Seth shrugged. "No matter what, you're still gonna be my little sibling. What matters is that you're happy. Are you happy?"

"I mean, a lot more than before."

"Then we're good. I'm just glad you finally admitted your feelings for Alex, that shit was getting painful to watch."

Wrinkling my nose, I reached across the counter and punched him in the arm. Not too hard, just enough so that he'd know he was being an asshole.

"Hey! You know I'm right."

Rolling my eyes, I let a little laugh escape me.

Quizzically, Alex looked over at Seth, "How long did you know?"

"A while, I think before Theo even realized it. It wasn't my place to tell you, so I just let it ride."

She shook her head in disbelief. "Damn, did everyone know except me?"

Seth snorted. "Probably."

I punched him again, harder this time. He almost dodged me, but he wasn't fast enough.

"I kid, I kid." He looked over at me more sympathetically. "I'm assuming Monica knows everything already?"

"Not...really. I think she knows about Alex but not," I gestured to myself, "this."

"Damn, you really went for it without telling her anything? Bold."

"I didn't really think about it. I didn't even realize you didn't know until I came down here."

"Oh, shit. Impulse to change got the better of you?"

"That was partially my fault," Alex joined in. "I was really excited and they told me a couple weeks ago while they were in the hospital, so I'd already gotten used to the idea. I didn't think about you or Monica either."

I dropped my fork on my plate and held my head. The thoughts were swarming again, like angry sharks to a drop of blood. "What if she hates me? I'm already enough of a disappointment. She took me in and all I've done is fuck things up, what if she doesn't want me anymore?" My inner thoughts and anxieties slipped out of me.

"Hey," Alex put a hand on the middle of my back. "Don't talk about yourself like that. She's okay with us, right? I don't see her being upset about this once she sees how much happier you are."

"I'm with Alex on this one, she barely batted an eye when I came out to her. She'll be cool with it, you'll see."

"I know it's scary," Alex lowered her voice to a softer tone. "But hey, at least you don't gotta come out to my mom." Her laugh was a hollow, empty sound. A chasm for her pain to fill. I hadn't even thought about her mom.

Alex's mom was the churchgoing holier-than-thou type — not the friendly "God loves everyone" kind either. She'd often made comments about how Mom was living in sin by not having a husband to help take care of her children. She'd never liked me — considered me little more than a piece of trash to be swept up on the street. She'd tolerated me when I was younger, but the uncomfortable dissonance when I was over led to Alex coming to my house more often than me going to hers. I think she preferred my house to get away from her mom anyway – the only thing keeping her there at all was her little sister. She loved that girl so much.

When I looked over at Alex, my heart cracked just a little around the edges. There were tears in her eyes. She'd left her hand on my back but dropped her own fork and was staring blankly in front of her. It was a look of desperation and fear I'd never wanted to see on her face.

"Alex…" I rested a hand on her cheek, brushing a tear away.

"She can never find out," she whispered, her voice wavering.

I pulled her face towards mine and kissed her forehead. Coming out to Mom sounded like a walk in the park compared to living with Alex's mother. I knew what it was like to feel unwanted, wrong. I never, ever wanted Alex to feel that. She cried softly in my arms as I brushed my hands through her long, wavy hair and kissed her face.

After a few minutes, she stopped, sitting up and wiping the tears from her face. "Sorry," she muttered.

"No, don't be. It's her that should be sorry." I ran a hand down her back. It was hard to mask the anger in my voice. "You're too good to feel so afraid of her. She should've never made you feel like that."

Why couldn't I believe my own words about myself?

She feigned a smile and rested a hand on my cheek. "You're too sweet, you know that?"

I hugged her and Seth cleared the plates that we no longer had any interest in. "Monica won't be home until morning, she's got a night shift tonight. You two'll have the house to yourselves. I'm going to practice with the band. Have fun." With a wink and his guitar case, he walked out the door.

I snorted in his direction. Things were about to be a lot more PG than he expected. I sat down on the couch and turned the TV on, and Alex flopped down next to me, putting her head in my lap and pulling my free arm down around her. We settled on a movie and I put my feet up on the coffee table. Is this what couples did? We'd always done this anyway, just with less cuddling. I laughed to myself.

"What?" She asked.

"I just realized, we were basically a couple before."

She laughed. A much fuller, rich sound this time. "I guess so."

I took a small section of her hair and started braiding it. She looked gorgeous with braids in her hair, taming the wild mess of red that it could become. Pulling it away from her face, I caught a glimpse of her bright green eyes.

"You're so beautiful," I whispered. Breathtaking.

She smiled her amazing smile, curled at the edges with half-closed eyes. I loved this. The calm, the sheer joy I felt just being with her. And yet, something gnawed at me, like I was afraid to be happy for once. She traced her hands along my arms, up to my neck, and pulled me down to her level for a kiss. My heart wasn't in it. Alex pulled away and opened her eyes.

"What's wrong?"

"I feel...guilty. Like I don't deserve this."

"You absolutely do." She ran her hand from my neck up to my hair.

"It just feels, I dunno, weird. I don't think anyone's ever really loved me before. At least not that I can remember. Not after my mom."

"Monica and Seth love you."

"No, they don't. Seth cares about me out of obligation and Mom's sister begged her to take me. No one's ever *chosen* me before. You could just get up and walk out any time you wanted, nothing's keeping you here."

"Theo, people having other reasons for staying doesn't mean that they don't love you. I'm here because I love you, but I also love you because you're a good friend and you're there for me when I need it."

"But like, they're supposed to, y'know? The position they're in means they're obligated to care…" I trailed off and stared at the TV for a minute, thinking of all the people who were "supposed" to have loved me in the past. "…Although I guess that obligation doesn't always mean people do it."

"See? There's a certain amount of love there, even if you don't always see it."

"You *chose* me though. You had plenty of other options, why did you choose me when we were little?"

"Honest? You looked miserable and your face is too cute for that. I wanted to make you smile. You deserve to smile."

I guess an eleven-year-old doesn't really need a thought out reason to make a friend. The real question though.

"Why did you stay?"

"You were so sweet – I could tell the toughness was just an act. I could see the real you and the real you is worth sticking around for."

She ruffled my hair again, slower this time. I took one of her hands and kissed it softly, then leaned against it with my face. She rubbed her hand against my cheek.

"I wish you would believe you're worth it."

A tear made its way down my face, wetting her hand. "I wish I could believe it too."

"One day you will. You'll see how special you are."

She brought my hand down to her chest, my fingers resting on her collarbone. We lost ourselves in the togetherness.

———

I awoke the next day hearing a clattering in the kitchen. Alex was still asleep in the bed next to me, and I carefully climbed over her and took a change of clothes to the bathroom. I changed out of the sports bra I'd worn to bed – Alex had done research and found that it was bad for you to sleep in a binder, otherwise I would've. She had to go and be sensible and worry about my health. I tried out the dinosaur underwear that was *so* much more comfortable than the panties I'd had before. I thought boxer briefs might've been kind of my thing. Then I put on the pair of boot-cut jeans and the koi t-shirt Alex had picked out. Finishing the ensemble with the dragon hoodie I'd been drawn to, I took a good look at myself in the mirror before brushing my teeth. Yesterday hadn't been a dream. I really did look so much different. I loved it.

A lump formed in my throat as I tip-toed down the stairs – Mom should be home. It was her that was the source of the clattering bang that had woken me up.

She heard me approach, but didn't look up from the pile of shattered ceramic that she was sweeping up. "Sorry I woke you sweetie, the cup practically jumped out of my hands."

She was always a little frazzled after her overnight shifts – not sleeping didn't suit her. She'd worked a double, too – she had already been gone when Alex and I had gotten home in the early afternoon. I felt bad, so I grabbed the dustpan to help her clean the mess up.

"Thank you."

She didn't seem to notice my appearance at first. In fact —
she made a whole 'nother cup of tea before she turned around and
really looked at me. At least it gave me time to try and stop shaking.

"Elizabeth!" Her voice was shrill and I flinched at the
sound of my old name.

She set the cup down before dropping it a second time and
came around the counter to get a better look. I awkwardly adjusted
my hoodie as my face got hotter and hotter.

Fuck. Fuck! She hates it. She hates me.

Trying to force the tears back, I started shaking even harder.

She caught the distress in my body language. "Oh sweetie,
no! I'm not upset with you. C'mere." She engulfed me in a warm
hug. Mom hugs were rare, she knew something was going on. "It's
just a big change is all."

"M-Mom, I'm…" I struggled to get the words out.

"I know you're dating Alex, sweetie. It's okay, you know
I'm bi, right?"

"No, I'm…wait, what?" Suddenly this wasn't just my
coming out.

"'Liz, I dated a woman for five months, she came over for
dinner a few times. You didn't notice?"

"I thought…" Had I really fallen for the old 'gal pals' trope?
I knew exactly who she was talking about now that she mentioned
it. Her "friend" Heather had been awfully chummy. Come to think
of it, she'd never said she was just a friend, but I don't think she
ever used the term "girlfriend" either. I stood there with my mouth
open like a fool, completely forgetting that *I* was supposed to be
coming out right now. Then again, she'd thought that I'd already
known, so was it really a coming out?

She laughed – a rich, musical sound. "You'll catch flies like that." She lightly placed her hand under my chin and closed my mouth. "Now, just because you're both girls doesn't mean you don't need protection, okay? I know that doesn't get taught in schools, I can get you what you need-"

"Mom, no." My face must've been beet red.

"Yes! I know Alex has had a few partners – there's no shame in that – but you need to be careful, in fact, we should get you both tested just to be safe—"

"Mom."

"Don't worry, I had the same talk with Seth when he had his first partner, it's not—"

I shook my head, trying to get back on track. Before she could keep going, I forced it out, "No, Mom. I'm trans."

She made a small squeak like she was about to say something else but my words had stopped her in her tracks. Her face fell a little, causing my heart to drop. Her posture stiffened, as if she didn't know how to react to the situation. My leg started bouncing as I sat down on one of the stools at the counter. She kept looking me over, studying me. I stared at my hands in my lap, avoiding eye contact, waiting for the yelling, the reprimands, the disowning. I expected a slap to the face. Something, anything other than this silence. Tears came, flowing down my face silently.

Mom broke from her frozen state and sat down next to me. She'd never seen me cry outside of that one day in the hospital. Not like this. She turned to me and put her hands over mine and took in a deep breath before speaking.

"I guess you'd like to be called something other than Liz?"

"Theo." My voice wavered a bit.

I couldn't tell if this was acceptance or if she was humoring me before throwing me out. I couldn't look her in the eyes to check. She placed a hand under my chin again, this time to lift my head to meet her eyes.

"Theo, you're precious to me, you know that? I know we don't always see eye to eye, but I've always loved you. You don't have to be my daughter to keep that."

Emotions flooded me and I couldn't stop the sob that forced its way out of me. I fell into her arms.

"Shh…" Mom rubbed my back as she held me.

After a minute, I sat up and dried my eyes on the sleeves of my hoodie. Sucking in a deep breath, I glanced up at her face, which held nothing but love. Alex was right, she did love me. I was foolish to think otherwise. Why else would she put up with everything I'd done and still show me so much compassion?

Still, I had to test it. "That's it? You're not mad?"

"Why would I be mad at you for being who you are? You've been unhappy for so long, I don't want you to force yourself to be something you're not for other people's sake. You deserve to be happy as yourself."

This was only a portion of my unhappiness falling away, but I felt so much lighter as it left me. Everyone I deeply cared about now knew and still loved me. Well, except Jeremy, but something told me he'd be okay with it. All the times I'd saved his ass, he owed me a little leeway.

Rubbing sleep from her eyes, Alex descended the stairs to find us in the kitchen. She looked at our faces and judged the situation with lightning speed.

"You told her?"

I nodded, trying to get the last bit of damp from my face with my sleeve.

"See? I told you she wouldn't be mad!"

Mom interjected, "She -er- he?"

"They?"

She nodded. "They didn't realize I'd had a girlfriend myself."

"What? Theo! Who did you think Heather was?"

Did everyone know except me?

"Shut up." I blushed, annoyed with how naive I'd been.

Mom tussled my hair and smiled. "I'm glad you told me."

––––––––––

Alex had to go home to placate her mother, so I'd texted Jeremy to hang out at the skate park for a bit. I wanted to skate, but this would be the first time I'd gone there since my attempt on my life, so I didn't want to do it alone. He was eager to hang out, it had been almost two months since he'd seen me. I hadn't had access to my phone in the hospital, so I'd left him hanging for a pretty long time.

I walked up to the gate, glancing across at the back alley where I'd done it. Standing frozen for a minute, my heart seemingly stopped as I tried to break out of the trance. This was where I'd nearly ended my life. Before I'd figured things out. I'd been so hopeless then, things were so different now. For the first time in my life I didn't want to give up on everything, and the fact that I'd nearly robbed myself of the chance to have this life still haunted me.

Before I could get too lost in the thought, Jeremy came jogging up to me. He'd beaten me here – not surprising, he lived closer.

"Liz! I barely recognized you!" He pointed up at my hair, and the slap in my face of my old name reminded me I had one last coming out to do. "I like it!" His grin was genuine. He'd missed me, I could tell. Sometimes I wondered if he had any other friends, it really didn't seem like it.

"Jer, we've got to talk."

His face fell a little, anxious at the tone of my voice. "You're right, we do."

I led us over to a more isolated corner of the park and leaned against the gate, dropping my skateboard to the ground and playing with it with my foot. He leaned next to me, concern written all over his face.

"It's nothing bad, I just…" I trailed off – this really didn't get any easier no matter how many times you did it. Suddenly, anxiety built up in me and I mulled over what his response would be, as if I could change it somehow with sheer willpower.

"Liz, whatever it is, it's okay."

I winced, "You've got to stop calling me that." The sting of the deadname hit me every single time, causing frustration to rise up and spill out in my words.

"Your...name?" He was confused. Rightly so, I hadn't told him anything.

"It's...it's Theo now. I'm not a girl."

His expression didn't change, although he appeared to be thinking over the information I'd given him. Finally, he came up with a response: "Makes sense."

"What do you mean?" My tone was short, offended at the idea that my previous terrible acting at being a girl hadn't been convincing. I don't know why that bothered me, but for some reason it did.

"I mean, I've never really been attracted to girls."

Oh, Jeremy, no.

I fell silent, not expecting that to be his reason.

"C'mon, L-Theo, you had to know. I wasn't good at hiding it. That's like, the number one reason Alex and I didn't get along really well. I was jealous of her."

"I...I didn't. Why are you telling me now?"

"Well, I figured since we're sharing…"

I rolled my eyes at him. He knew I didn't feel the same way, it was written all over his face. I felt a little bad, knowing how it felt to hold something like that in for so long, and then the devastation of a lack of reciprocation.

"S'okay, please just tell me you told Alex in all of this? I hate watching you fawn over her – she loves you too, I know it."

"We're actually...a thing now, I guess."

"You guess?"

"We are. We're together."

He slapped my shoulder with a genuine grin I don't think I could ever muster if I'd been in his position. "Good. I just want you to be happy."

"That's what everyone keeps saying."

"Because it's true! You live stuck in your head so much, I don't think you realize how much people care about you."

I shrugged, knowing he was right but unwilling to admit it to him.

"So what, you just drop off the face of the earth for two months and come back a new person? What happened?"

Shit. He doesn't know.

"No one told you?"

"I don't really talk to anyone else. Seth offered to hang out a couple times, but I couldn't get anything out of him. I thought it was a little weird that he'd offer to chill out of nowhere like that."

Sliding to the ground, I sighed heavily. This was a whole

different kind of coming out.

In a much less dramatic fashion, he sat down next to me, looking on expectantly. He wasn't going to let me get out of this.

"Jer...I tried to kill myself. I was in the hospital."

His face twisted in a way that said he was trying not to cry. "Are you serious?"

"I wouldn't lie about that." I couldn't look at him, I was trying too hard to keep a stoic expression on my face. In all of this, he was one of the only people that hadn't seen me cry. I was a protector to him – I didn't want cracks in that facade too.

Even without looking at him, I could feel his desperation, "But...why...how…" He ended the incomplete thought with a sniffle.

"I don't want to talk about that. I'm doing a lot better now, I promise."

He rested a hand on my knee. "You're sure?"

I managed a glance in his direction before looking away again. "Very. I'm the best I've ever been."

"I knew...I knew you were struggling. All the drugs, the drinking. I just didn't know how to help."

Patting his back, I offered, "you did your best. You kept me safe when you could. I'm sorry I dragged you into so much shit. I'm done with it, I'm not going back."

"You dragged me out of more shit than you dragged me into, promise." His expression was cold, distant.

Shit, no one's been there to take care of him.

"Things at home been bad while I've been gone?"

He shrugged, "Like I said, Seth offered to hang out a few times. Otherwise it's been the usual."

There were bruises lining his upper arms, and he tugged his sleeve down when he saw me looking.

"So, bad," I said.

He nodded slowly, avoiding my eyes.

"You know you can still come to my house whenever, right? I'm sorry I wasn't there for so long. I did tell Seth to look out for you."

Guilt washed over me. I'd been such a bad friend.

"No. No, don't feel bad. You had your own shit you needed to get straight. I'm not upset with you for taking care of yourself. There's nothing wrong with that. You can't always take care of everyone, Theo."

"I guess...I just feel like I let you down."

"Nah," he waved his hand in the air, "you just got out of the hospital, right? You didn't let anyone down. You survived. Now, if you'd died, then I'd have been pissed." There was a slight laugh at the end of his phrase, trying to lighten the mood.

I gave him the laugh he was hoping for and pushed his shoulder slightly, avoiding the bruises.

"I will take you up on that offer to come over though, my mom was drinking before I even left. I was considering a park bench for a minute."

"We skate first though, right?" I was itching to feel the wind on my face.

He held up a fist for me to pound. "We skate first."

CHAPTER FIFTEEN

With Jeremy asleep on the couch downstairs, Alex came back to my house and we made our way upstairs. We'd have to go to school tomorrow, which I wasn't looking forward to. I'd be pounced on the minute I walked in the door. I'd like to say I didn't know how people would react to the change. The truth was, I knew exactly how they'd react, and that was the problem. There would be scoffing and shoving and maybe even some punching. I could take it, but my fear was that I'd react beyond pushing people away. I'd gotten my anger under control significantly more than it had been the day I'd been arrested, but I still had my breaking point. Hopefully Alex being there could deter any rash reactions.

Alex wasn't focused on school, now. The minute we got up to my room she'd dropped her bag for tomorrow in the corner and turned to me with a longing in her eyes. A hunger, even – one I didn't understand until she walked right up to me and ran her hands down my back, pulling me close to her. Our faces were less than an inch apart as she started kissing me.

Suddenly, we were moving across my room and onto my bed. I embraced her back and ran my hands through her long, wavy hair. Alex held me tight as I leaned into her kiss. We were pressed up against the corner of my bed – we couldn't physically get any closer together but I ached to be closer still. She ran her hands through my hair and I wrapped my arms around her back. I didn't want to let go of the kiss, but Alex leaned back and in one swift motion, pulled her shirt off.

"Is this okay?" she asked.

My heart skipped a beat as I looked at her bare chest and nodded. This was a new feeling, one I'd never had before. An ache to be closer with her than ever before. She leaned back into me, and I felt her warmth against me. That was the best part – her skin touching mine. I never wanted it to end. Alex put her hands under my shirt and ran them along my stomach. I felt exposed, but not in a bad way. My head felt light, dizzy. I took in a sharp breath when suddenly Alex pulled her hands away.

"Theo?"

"Mm?" I looked at her through half closed eyes.

"Theo, stop."

I froze. Immediately, I took my hands off of her and opened my eyes. Did I do something wrong? Did I hurt her?

Fuck, I couldn't even get this right.

"You're crying."

"What?" My hands flew up to my face and they came away wet.

What the fuck?

"Fuck...shit, I'm sorry."

"Honey, don't be sorry. What's wrong?"

"I...I don't know. I don't know why I'm crying. What...the fuck?"

It was amazing how quickly all the good feelings were being replaced with frustration and confusion. I started shaking. Alex ran her hands down my bare arms. The touch still felt good and I wanted more. Didn't I? She wiped the tears away from my face and more came rushing down. She kissed my forehead softly and a sob escaped me – I didn't understand. She sat up and pulled my head down into her chest as I started crying harder. I was so embarrassed and I didn't understand why my body was betraying me like this. Alex stroked my hair and I wrapped my arms tightly around her. I still didn't want to let go.

"Somebody hurt you, didn't they?" Her voice was barely a whisper. There was an ache in her tone like it hurt her to say.

I was brought back to an unforgiving mattress with a history of agony where I clutched a kitchen knife and waited for him to come to me. My small hands made the knife look monumentally large. It had been enough, he wouldn't hurt me again. Tonight would be the end of it.

The tears were coming hard and fast now. My shaking seemingly moved both of us, and my grip around Alex's waist was so tight that I feared I'd hurt her. If she was uncomfortable, she didn't show it. She just held me and let me cry.

"It's okay if you're not ready. It'll be okay if you're never ready. Don't feel bad, I don't need this to love you."

"I really wanted it," I choked out.

"It's okay, honey." She cooed and held me tighter.

My breathing eventually began to slow and I was able to stop the tears. I pulled my shirt off, revealing the black half-tank binder I'd been wearing as often as possible since yesterday. Alex gave me a confused look, but embraced me as I laid back down in her arms.

"Can we just...lie like this for a while?" I wanted the feeling of her skin on mine as much as possible.

"Of course."

————————

I grumbled the next morning as my alarm went off. I wasn't used to getting up this early anymore, and some of the meds I'd been given made me groggy in the morning. Alex rolled out of bed before me, gathering up a fresh change of clothes from her backpack and leaving for the bathroom.

Pulling myself up by the shelves lining my bed, I sat and blinked for a minute before putting my glasses on. I was met with the three different medication bottles I'd been prescribed. Right, I'd have to take those. Mom had given me one of those weekly pill sorter things that had different slots for morning and night so that I wouldn't get confused and end up sleeping my way through school. I picked it up and opened the Monday morning container and took it with a sip from the bottle of water I'd left next to all the meds.

I dragged myself out of bed and stumbled a bit, still feeling a little dizzy. I made my way over to my dresser where I pulled out my binder and one of my new t-shirts, along with some jeans. Sitting down in my desk chair, I rubbed my eyes as I waited for Alex to get out of the bathroom. Sure, there was another bathroom downstairs, but that was *so far away*. The longer I didn't have to do anything, the better. God, and I used to be a morning person. If that was all I had to trade for how much better I'd felt overall, I supposed it was worth it. Hell, ditching the nightmares alone was worth it.

Alex came back to my room, looking entirely too well made-up for the ten minutes she'd spent in the bathroom. She smiled at me and tousled my already messed-up hair. She was never a morning person like I had been, but apparently in comparison to my energy level she was now. I got up and staggered into the bathroom, splashing cold water on my face in an attempt to wake up. It helped a little, but my eyelids still felt heavy and there were deep dark circles under my eyes. More cold water. Hell, maybe a cold shower. I hopped in and made the water as cold as I could bear until I finally started to feel more awake.

As I got out, I dried myself off and started getting ready. Whoever said putting on jeans after a shower was difficult certainly never tried to put a binder on right out of the shower. I contorted and twisted, pulling at the fabric until, after expelling an incredible amount of energy, I finally got it where it was supposed to be. Sucking in a deep breath, I leaned forwards and stared at myself in the mirror. My face was reddened by all the effort I'd just put into getting a piece of clothing on, but hey, the dark circles had lightened up some. I was a mess. I didn't feel ready to go back to school.

A knock on the door. "You okay, hun?"

"Yeah," I muttered.

"We've got ten minutes."

Ugh.

I got the rest of my clothes on much quicker and made an attempt to straighten out my hair, then grabbed my backpack out of my room and trudged down the stairs.

The house was like a cafe. Jeremy and Alex were both sitting on stools at the counter eating, Seth at the stove finishing off some eggs and throwing them onto a plate for me. Mom was leaning against the sink drinking a cup of coffee.

I sat down on the stool next to Alex as Seth set a plate

in front of me – an egg sandwich with ham, my favorite. Eating quickly, I nodded in Alex and Jeremy's direction.

"You two getting along okay now?"

"Yeah, we talked a bit." Jeremy nodded.

Alex gave him a smile, not the fake one she usually sent in his direction either. At least I didn't have to worry about them bickering when I wasn't there anymore.

Leaning towards me, Alex started fixing my hair while I ate. "You didn't even dry it, did you?"

"M…no." I said through a mouth full of food.

She shook her head at me and grabbed a dish towel, drying off my hair and then fluffing it upwards to mimic the style the hairdresser had done when she'd cut it. My hair curled a little at the ends now that it wasn't weighed down with water and Alex continued arranging it until she was satisfied.

Mom nodded at me. "Sweetie, I know today's going to be tough. If it gets to be too much, just go to the nurse and have her call me, okay? I already talked with her, they shouldn't give you any trouble for that."

A little embarrassed that my mom had to make an escape plan for me, I nodded. I was grateful at the same time for the option to bail out if needed. It made the day feel a little less daunting. I'd try my best, but my best only got me so far sometimes.

The bus approached the house and the four of us ran out the door with our bags. Seth and Jeremy on first, Alex and I right after. Eyes darted in my direction and the whispers started already. I ignored them and followed Alex to a seat towards the back.

The kids behind us laughed and one even leaned forward to touch my hair. "What the fuck is this?"

Before I could even respond, Alex was on her feet and

slapped the kid's hand away. "Fuck off, Rory."

Rory did indeed fuck off.

Amused by Alex's sudden protectiveness, I laughed and grabbed her hand as she sat back down. She smiled at me and fixed my hair again.

These kids weren't even the ones I was worried about. It was that one group – the one that always hassled Jeremy – that could push me until I snapped. I didn't want to snap. I wanted to have a good day and just focus on classes.

God, who am I?

Getting through the day without incident was my first priority. Anything beyond that would be a bonus.

Once the bus arrived, we waited for all the other kids to get off before leaving. Maybe hanging back would mean missing the group of kids I didn't want to run into. Unlikely, though, they were always hanging around in the halls. It was a wonder they weren't in trouble more often for missing or being late to classes.

Alex interlaced her fingers with mine as we walked in the front door of the school. Lo and behold, there they were.

Fuck.

As if he had radar pinged specifically for me, the leader of the group turned his attention and approached us.

"Now what's this?"

He shoved me, knocking me into Alex.

We tried to ignore him and keep walking, but him and his little gang stepped in front of us.

"Of course little Lizzie here is a dyke! We should've known!"

He pushed me again, and I let go of Alex's hand, not wanting to pull her backwards with me. The group started cackling and Alex stepped between us.

"Just leave them alone."

"And what're you going to do about it, slut? Clearly you'll jump anything that moves, you don't even care if it's got a dick!"

Anger boiled up in me and my face got hotter and hotter. I didn't care so much when he was insulting me, but calling Alex names made me want to strike. Dropping my bag, I rolled up the sleeves of my hoodie.

Alex whirled to face me. "Theo, don't."

Right. I was supposed to make better choices. Not let them get to me.

"What's the matter? Too pussy to fight me now?"

God, it would feel so good to punch his rat face right now. I sucked in a deep breath and picked my bag back up, grabbed Alex by the arm, and walked straight through them, pushing them out of the way so fast a couple of them almost fell.

"Hey! We're not done!"

Yes, we are.

Alex put a hand on my back and kissed my cheek. "Good job, hun."

It did feel kind of good to walk away and leave them looking like a bunch of assholes. They couldn't take pleasure in riling me up if I wasn't there.

We split up to go to our separate classes, and I stopped at my English teacher's desk.

"Elizabeth! It's been a bit, how are you doing?"

Ugh, now I had to do this with every teacher. I knew some of them wouldn't understand and I thought about just letting the deadname go in those classes, the confrontation not worth the stress and unlikely to get them to change anyway. This one, at least, was worth it. The only teacher I'd go to with anything.

"Actually...could, could you call me Theo?"

Her eyes scanned me and took in my new appearance. I fidgeted a little, unsure of what her reaction would be, but very much needing it to be a good one. After a minute, she smiled at me.

"Of course, Theo. Would you like me to use different pronouns?"

"They/them."

She nodded. "Okay, I can do that. I might mess up a bit at first, but I promise to do my best."

Relief washed over me and I managed to smile and nod back at her before finding my seat. The glares from my classmates didn't touch me, I didn't care what they thought.

The rest of the class was uneventful, aside from some whispers around me. Were people's lives really so boring that they had to focus on me so much? What a sad reality. After the bell rang, I waited for everyone to leave before approaching the teacher again.

"Thank you. For being kind. You're the only teacher that likes me."

She turned around from erasing the blackboard and offered me a smile. "High school's tough, you've gotta have someone in your corner. Plus your writing has so much potential – more than you realize. I look forward to reading your work again."

I smiled back at her, feeling my cheeks get hot. I wasn't used to compliments on my work. Most teachers assumed I was headed to prison or the streets and not worth their time.

"You believe in me."

"Of course I do." She offered me a hug and to both of our surprise, I took it.

Now it was time to face every other shitty teacher in this hellhole. Next was the math teacher that always assumed I was failing on purpose. I'd already decided I wasn't going to go out of my way to talk to him. Let him call me the wrong name. The argument wasn't worth it.

The other worst part of that class – the group of hecklers was in it. Hopefully they'd skip the class and I wouldn't have to deal with them.

Walking in the room, I saw they hadn't skipped. They were punctual, even – the bell hadn't rung yet. I sat as far away from them as I could but the jeers started as soon as I walked in the room.

"Hey, pussy dyke! Who you gonna hide behind now that your slutty girlfriend isn't here?"

I clenched my fists and jaw, trying to ignore them. As long as they didn't put their hands on me, I'd be okay. Words were easy enough to ignore. Plus, their insults were pathetic. It was like they just strung together as many obscenities as they could think of until they came out in a barely coherent sentence.

They started chanting, "Pussy dyke! Pussy dyke!"

Sucking in a deep breath, I held it and then let it out like I'd learned in the hospital. The teacher looked up from his laptop, but didn't address the kids. He glanced at me, as if trying to gauge when I'd explode on them. When the situation would become dangerous.

The leader of the group got up and walked over to me. The teacher's eyes followed him, but still he was silent. That's when the kid walked right up to my desk, spit in my face, and then ran away.

Without thinking, I stood up so fast that my chair fell down behind me. My fists were primed and ready to go.

"Elizabeth!" The teacher shouted.

I couldn't keep the thought inside. "Are you fucking serious? You just watched him do that."

"And you're about to put your hands on him. If there's one

thing I don't tolerate, it's violence."

I grabbed my backpack and turned towards the exit. "I'm going to the bathroom." I forced out in a growl. The group was laughing and high-fiving like a bunch of petty children, and I could almost hear the teacher rolling his eyes.

Once I was out of the room, I ran the rest of the way to the bathroom. I splashed cold water on my face, trying to get the kid's disgusting slime off. He probably didn't even brush his teeth. My hand shook and my face was bright red. I tried taking some deep, measured breaths. Was it time to tap out? How much more of this could I take? It was only the second class of the day. I was a little disappointed in myself for not making it longer.

Maybe I'd just take a little break. Yeah, a break sounded better. I remembered that the doctor had given me a prescription I could take as needed when I felt too agitated, although I didn't bring it. Hopefully Mom had thought ahead and given some to the nurse.

I decided to take the chance and walked to the nurse's station. The nurse offered me a warm smile and stood up from her desk when I walked into the office.

"Hey, Theo. Do you want me to call your mom?"

The use of the right name actually floored me, and I blinked up at her for a second. "How...?"

"Your mom and I had a chat early this morning, told me your name and everything. One less person you've got to tell, right?"

I nodded slowly, glad more than just my English teacher was accepting.

"So, would you like me to call her?"

"No. I...did she give you any meds for me?"

"As a matter of fact, she did! Dropped them off about twenty minutes ago." She pulled a bottle out of a locked glass case that had a bunch of different student medications inside. She showed it to me. "This what you're looking for?"

I glanced at the bottle. Ativan. I hadn't remembered the name of most of my medications, but I trusted Mom to have brought the right one. Plus, I remembered them giving the same med to Sam when she'd had her panic attack. I nodded at the nurse and she took out a pill and put it in a small disposable cup – it reminded me of the hospital. She filled another cup with water and then handed them to me. I took them, my hands still shaking so badly I almost spilled the water on its way to my mouth. The nurse noticed and came out from behind her desk. She guided me to a small couch and had me sit down.

"What's got you so upset?"

"Kid spit in my face."

"What?!"

I pulled in another deep breath. "Teacher didn't give a shit. I'm the one who got yelled at."

She shook her head, "That's not right. What class was this?"

"Math."

She furrowed her eyebrows and held up a finger as she walked back behind her desk and picked up a phone. I didn't really listen, my vision was tunneling and I was shaking harder. My face still felt hot, and then it was just my eyes. I was crying.

What the fuck?

I hated how easily I cried lately. Lifting my glasses, I wiped my eyes as my leg started bouncing up and down so fast it felt like I might take off into the ceiling. The nurse came back a minute later.

"You sure you don't want me to call your mom?"

I didn't know anymore. Still, I shook my head no.

"You can wait here until you feel better, take your time."

Her voice tried to soothe me, "I'm glad you came here instead of lashing out – your mom's right, you have made a lot of progress. Not too long ago I was patching up your knuckles."

I kept trying to take breaths, until eventually the agitation inside me started to die down. Now I really felt like crying. I was *tired* and had no idea if it was from being overwhelmed with emotion or the meds. Either way, I just wanted to sleep.

"Hey," The nurse's tone was low and soft, "You know there's no shame in taking the tap out, right? Sometimes you've got to take care of yourself. You've made a lot of progress but you also haven't been in this setting for two months. It's a lot. Not making it all the way through the first day isn't something to be ashamed of. You should be proud that you came at all, and you tried really hard."

Tears came, I didn't try to stop them. Why couldn't everyone be this understanding? It would make things a lot easier.

Finally, I relented. "Call my mom, please."

Mom showed up probably fifteen minutes later – the hospital wasn't far from the school. I felt bad that I'd made her come from work.

"You all right, sweetie?" She asked, sitting down on the couch and laying an arm around me.

My eyes were still red and puffy from crying, and I leaned into her.

"There was an incident with another student." The nurse offered.

Mom's eyes fell on me. "Did you hit anyone?"

"No, I didn't do anything. Just walked out, and then I got really overwhelmed. I took an Ativan but now I'm really tired and everything feels like too much."

"Good job, sweetie. I know that's hard. How about we go home and you get a nap in before therapy?"

Therapy. I'd forgotten that I had therapy. I nodded, Mom said thank you to the nurse and then led me out of the school to the car. She brought me home and then sat me on the couch, making tea for both of us.

"Will you be all right here for a bit? I've got to get back to work."

"Yeah, I'm just gonna take a nap." I sipped the tea. Chamomile always put me to sleep.

She pulled a blanket over me and rested a hand on my shoulder before grabbing her keys and walking out the door. I turned on some cartoons and within minutes was asleep.

———

I awoke to the front door closing and a weight on the end of the couch. Opening my eyes slightly, I saw Alex drop her bag and then lean back on the couch, letting out an exasperated sigh. Pushing myself up, I put the blanket over her too and leaned on her shoulder.

"Was it just as bad for you?" I asked, finding her hand with mine.

"That place is such a shithole. I'm glad me and Jeremy are cool now, otherwise I would've been eating in the bathroom."

"I'm sorry I wasn't there." I traced circles in her palm.

"No, you gotta take care of yourself, that's more important. What happened anyway?"

"Kid spit in my face."

"Oh no, Theo, you didn't…"

"I didn't do anything but walk out. I got really overwhelmed after and couldn't do it then."

"Oh, I'm so glad you didn't do anything! You're really strong, you know that? It takes real strength to walk away."

"Do you think it'll ever get better?"

She clasped her hand around mine. "I hope so, this shit is exhausting."

Mom walked in the door a few minutes later. "Hey, kiddos. You feeling any better, sweetie?" She set her keys down and grabbed a glass of water.

"A little."

"Good. We've got to leave for your appointment in a few, okay?"

"Ugh."

I wasn't looking forward to starting everything over with a new therapist. I'd have to rehash everything, and that was incredibly exhausting. Hopefully Carmen had passed on some notes or something so I didn't have to tell the new therapist *everything*.

"It'll be okay," Alex said softly, running her free hand through my hair. "We can just chill after, I'll make you something to eat while you're gone."

Pushing myself up off the couch, I gave Alex a kiss before trudging over to the door and putting on my shoes. Mom herded me out the door and shot a smile in Alex's direction on the way out.

"Don't burn the place down."

Alex snickered. We all knew that would be Mom's doing, she's the one who couldn't boil water.

We drove in a comfortable silence to the office where my new therapist was. I sat down in a waiting-room chair and fidgeted while Mom checked me in. There was a small noise machine outside the door, a few books and toys for younger kids to use while waiting. I wondered if this therapist mostly worked with little kids. I hoped not, the condescending "kiddie" voice that adults used grated on my nerves.

After a few minutes, the door opened and a woman a bit taller than me stepped out. She had light brown skin and thick, natural hair that was pulled back into a bun. Her clothes were a little more professional looking than Carmen's had been – I suppose she was fancier in having her own office instead of working out of a hospital.

"Theo?" she asked.

Mom waved me away and I got up slowly to cautiously follow the woman. She led me back to an office that was covered in colorful drawings that looked like they'd been done by children. I sat down on the couch that she had and she sat across from me in a tall plush chair.

"Hello, Theo. I'm Louise. Let's see if we'd be a good fit to work together, okay? Is it all right if I ask you a few questions?"

I nodded. Her office screamed that children were her focus, but at least she didn't use an obnoxious baby voice when talking to me. She just talked like I was a human. It was that same trait that I'd liked about Carmen, so many medical professionals talking down to me throughout my life made it clear what most of them thought of me.

"So you've got some tentative diagnoses here of PTSD, depression, and anxiety. What feels like it causes you the most distress in your daily life?"

"I...uh...I get overwhelmed really easily. I had to leave school today because I got so overwhelmed."

"What happens in your body when you get overwhelmed?"

"I get hot and shaky, and sometimes really angry. Sometimes I can't control the anger. It's gotten me in trouble before, I've hurt people."

"Hurt people physically or emotionally?"

"Physically. When I'm mad my brain doesn't do words so well."

"I see." She pushed her thick-rimmed glasses up her nose.

"The angry part's been better since I got meds, now I get more tired than mad."

"Are you better able to handle your anger?"

"Yeah. I don't get as lost in it."

"Good, good. What kind of situations do you get overwhelmed in?"

"Mostly when people touch me or threaten me. People don't really like me so I get a lot of that."

"Do you feel like it's a defensive action when you're overwhelmed by being touched?"

"Yeah. I want people to leave me alone."

She scribbled something down in her notes. "Make sense."

I fidgeted with my hands as she fell silent for a minute, thinking.

"Okay, tell me a little about yourself. What kinds of things make you happy?"

"Uh...I like skateboarding. My English teacher says I'm good at writing."

"Are you interested in writing?"

"A little. Carmen had me write stuff when I got upset and it helped a little."

"Good! Do you have any supports?"

"What?"

"Supports – people you can talk to."

"My...my girlfriend. And my mom I guess."

She smiled, "How long have you been with your girlfriend?"

"Like six weeks, I guess. But we've been friends for four years."

"So she's been in your life a long time."

"Yeah."

"Okay, Theo. Carmen told me you found it helpful to play a game or do something with your hands while you were talking. Would you like to pick out a game while we dive in for the day?"

"Okay."

She showed me to a shelf that was loaded with even more games than Carmen had. I picked something simple – not sure how long I'd last in the session. I was already tired. Uno seemed good enough. I shuffled and then she dealt out the cards, flipping over the top card of the deck.

"So, why don't we talk about what happened at school to make you leave today? Can you tell me what happened?"

"There's this group of kids that picks on almost everyone – I used to fight them a lot so when I came in today looking like, well, me...they went straight for me. I walked away from them the first time but then I had a class with them and one of them spit in my face and the teacher didn't do anything."

There was a slight downward twitch on Louise's lips when I'd finished explaining, but she kept whatever comment had flashed through her mind to herself. "How did you respond when he spit on you?"

"I got up really fast. I think I was going to hit him but the teacher yelled at me."

"So the teacher addressed you before you'd done anything, but didn't say anything to the kid that spit in your face?"

A scowl overtook my face. "Yeah."

"Well that's...pretty shitty. I don't blame you for getting overwhelmed. What did you do next?"

My face loosened after she talked. I didn't think I'd ever heard a therapist swear before, it was kind of funny to me. "I walked out and went to the nurse to get the med I'm supposed to take when I get agitated."

"Good use of tools that you have available to you – it sounds like you did a really good job there."

"I got really hot and shaky and started crying in the nurse's office, that's when we called my mom."

"It kind of makes sense that you would. You're used to releasing all the adrenaline physically by fighting. When you don't fight, it has nowhere to go. Maybe in the meantime while you're learning to handle that adrenaline, doing something physical might help? Going for a walk or something?"

"Maybe..."

"I know that might not always be available to you, but it's a thought for when it is."

"Yeah..." I leaned back, dropping my last card. I'd forgotten to say uno, but the game didn't really matter anyway. It never did.

She picked up the cards and started shuffling. A smooth, rhythmic sound. "Is there anything else you'd like to talk about?"

My mind flashed to me and Alex the night before. I wanted to figure out what happened, but I was embarrassed to talk about sex in general, let alone with someone I'd just met.

"I uh...I...hm." I couldn't get it out.

"Don't worry Theo, nothing leaves this office. I'm not going to judge you on anything. I'm just a neutral party here to help you figure things out."

"Alex and I ...we..." God damn, this was hard.

Louise waited patiently. I wasn't getting out of this now that I'd started.

"We tried to do...*stuff*...last night. And I wanted to, I really did. But I started crying without even realizing it. I didn't know I was until she got worried and made me stop. I still don't know why I started crying but then I had a flashback after."

"I see. Have you ever had sex before?"

I cringed at the word, but shook my head. "I don't think so...not...not when I wanted it."

"Ah." The implication clicked in her head. She tapped her chin, "Do you feel safe with Alex?"

"Yes. More than I ever have with anyone else."

She fell silent for a minute, finally dealing out the cards.

"Do you know what happened?" I asked, hopeful for answers.

She pulled in a deep breath. "It might be a trauma response."

"But I didn't have a flashback until after."

"You don't necessarily need to have a flashback – your body remembers trauma, too. Even though in the moment you wanted to do it and felt safe, your body's never had that kind of touch be a good thing. So when it happens, it remembers the bad things even if *you* aren't necessarily remembering them."

"Oh." I stared down at my cards for a few minutes. "Will it ever go away?"

"It'll take time. You might need to take it slow and check in – tell yourself it's okay, that you're safe."

"It's really frustrating. I felt so bad."

"How did Alex respond?"

"She just had me stop and then held me. She tries to make

me feel better all the time."

"So this may be a conversation you have to have with her. It sounds like she'd be open to figure out what you need in the situation."

"Yeah," I squinted, "I guess."

"It can be a tough conversation to have, but if you want to be intimate with her, I think it would be worthwhile."

"Okay." Another conversation I wasn't looking forward to. Why did everything have to be so difficult?

"We can try and work through some stuff in here, if you feel like you're ready to take that dive. I know Carmen said that's a topic you had a difficult time with."

Things were starting to feel fuzzy. "No...not yet." I was too exhausted. All I wanted to do was go back to sleep. "Can...can we be done? I'm really tired."

"I think you've done some really good work today, and it's just about time anyway. So yes, I'll see you next week."

She smiled at me and walked me out the door back to the waiting room where mom was sitting. Mom and Louise nodded at each other in some unspoken doctor language and then Mom guided me back out to the car.

We began the drive back home when I asked, "Mom, can I stay home tomorrow? I'll go on Wednesday. I just feel like I need to sleep forever. I don't feel good."

She gave me a concerned glance out of the corner of her eyes, staying fixated on the road. "I thought this might be a lot, going back and having your first appointment the same day. We can take it slow, but you've missed a lot of school. We might need to get you a tutor."

"Okay." I didn't have the energy to argue.

Besides, a tutor didn't sound so bad. I could do the work minus the shouted insults in the hallway and getting spit on.

———————

I slept all the way through until noon the next day. When I woke up, I hurriedly took my meds – I was supposed to take them in the morning, oops. At least I felt a little bit better, not quite as groggy and a lot less stressed. Trudging down the stairs, I opened the fridge to find French toast that Seth had made in the morning with my name on it. I stuck it in the microwave and got out some butter and syrup, my stomach growling in the process. I hadn't eaten dinner the night before because I'd gone straight back to bed after my therapy session. I didn't even know if Alex had stayed the night or not, I felt a little bad for that.

Taking out my phone, I scrolled through to find a message from Alex.

Good morning sleepy! I love you, hope you're feeling better today.

A grin cracked across my face and I texted her a "love you" back. The microwave beeped, so I took out the hot plate and then devoured the toast without even sitting down. After I'd washed my plate, I flopped down on the couch and turned on the tv, curling up with the blanket. I still felt like I could sleep more.

Eventually, the door opened and Alex walked in, Seth following her. Mom wouldn't be home for a few more hours. Alex fell down on the couch and wrapped her arms around me.

"You feeling better today?"

"Yeah. How was school?"

"A little better than yesterday. I think the kids will get their bullshit out of their system by the end of the week if we're lucky."

"I'm sorry you have to go through this shit because of me."

"No! Don't be sorry for other people's ignorance. That's not your fault. Plus, I'd gladly deal with it every day if that means I get to be with you." She planted a kiss on my forehead and I leaned into her, burying my face in her chest.

Seth went up the stairs, too focused on what he was doing to even acknowledge me. Once I heard his door shut and his guitar start playing, I turned to Alex.

"Al, we have to talk about what happened."

She quirked an eyebrow at me. "What happened?"

"The other night when we...you know." I didn't even like saying it with her.

"Ooh. It's okay – like I said, we can wait until you're ready."

"That's the thing, I talked to my therapist about it a little and...I don't know if I *can* be ready without practice? She said that my body remembers trauma and it's not used to that kind of touch being a good thing, so I think I gotta like...make it used to it somehow?"

Alex tapped her forehead with her index finger. "I get you. So we just gotta take it really, really slow. That's okay."

"I still don't really even know what to do. I've never wanted to do it with anyone else, ever. But I want to with you."

She kissed my forehead. "I want to with you too, but I want it to be good for both of us. I'll do whatever you need. We'll work on it together."

I put my head down in her lap and looked up at her, placing a hand on her cheek. "I love you."

"I love you too, T."

EPILOGUE

When I started this journey, I never would've thought that things would end up the way that they did. I'd had some significantly tough times, but to get where I am I wouldn't trade it for the world. I'm in a place now where I can see my life has value – a lot of things are still a struggle for me, but I don't feel so alone anymore. I have help, help that I've needed for a long time.

If it's a comfort or a lesson to anyone, I want them to know that it's okay to need that help. It's something I struggled with for so long – wanting to do things all on my own, avoid all the pain that wracked my life. Sometimes the only way out is through. It's a cliche, I know. But it's one I've found to be true. My life's been a struggle, but I feel like sometimes we're all struggling, vying to find our place in the world.

I've known pain and sorrow and incredible guilt, but I've also found love. The secrets we keep can slowly kill us – sometimes they need to be let out, no matter how painful. It's difficult to find the people to trust with these secrets. Those people do exist, and I've found them.

You'll find your people. Even if the family you're born into isn't it. Found family is just as – if not more – valid and important. I didn't find my family until I was twelve and even then I didn't learn to let them in until I was sixteen. No matter how long it takes, you will find those you're meant to be with.

We all deserve love and companionship, even when we feel like we don't. It's tough to accept sometimes, but once you learn to accept the love that's out there for you, it can be such a freeing experience. Who you are doesn't disqualify you from this love, it's who you are that lets you claim this love. While you might feel like you're not worth it, don't ever believe that voice in your head. It's a liar. You deserve love. You're worthy of it. You're a beautifully imperfect person who has a lot to give, even if you don't feel like it. Imperfection is what makes us valuable.

Above all else, I'll love you. You can be part of my family. Everyone has a place here.